THE BIGGEST HEART EVER

Arlie Undercover, Book 2

Dani Haviland

USA Today Bestselling Author

The Biggest Heart Ever and the *Arlie Undercover* series are works of fiction. Names, place, characters, and incidents are the product of the author's imagination and are used for the readers' enjoyment. Any resemblance to persons living, dead, or fictional, events or business establishments is entirely coincidental.

ISBN 978-1-946752-22-2

Book Description

While recuperating from the bullet he received in the line of duty, Arlie Biggar—known as Daywalker or Charles Baggar to the criminals he harassed as an Anchorage undercover detective—finds a new love in sunny Arizona. When he brings his new family back to wintertime Alaska, unexpected dangers await the officer still on medical leave.

Arlie Undercover Series

Arlie Biggar is a dedicated undercover detective who creates fantastic apps and devices to help him capture the bad guys. Life gets complicated when he suddenly has a family to take care of—and keep safe from a gang of angry mobsters.

A Stingray Christmas (Book One in the series)

Arlie was content to forgo having a personal life, but the Alaskan detective couldn't give up on 'stalking' the woman who had received his deceptive one-time sperm donation. A medical leave to sunny Arizona reveals a life-changing surprise he hadn't counted on…and an unexpected attraction to the mother of his son.

Acknowledgment

Many thanks to my editor, Elaine Boyle, for suggesting I give Arlie more than a one-shot appearance (A Stingray Christmas). Thanks to my Anchorage friend, police officer John Daily, for making sure I don't take too much poetic license with Arlie, my tenacious—and very techno-clever—undercover detective. Thanks to John and all the others who serve and protect!

Chapter 1
Christmas Eve

Banner Hospital
Mesa, Arizona

News article: Opioids are a class of drugs that include the illicit drug heroin as well as the licit prescription pain relievers oxycodone, hydrocodone, codeine, morphine, fentanyl and others. Drug overdose is the leading cause of accidental death in the US, with 52,404 lethal drug overdoses in 2015. Opioid addiction is driving this epidemic, with 20,101 overdose deaths related to prescription pain relievers, and 12,990 overdose deaths related to heroin in 2015. 2016 Opioid Addiction Facts and Figures from the American Society of Addiction Medicine.

"I really don't want to take anything this strong. Good ol' Ibuprofen or aspirin will work fine for me. And if it doesn't, maybe I'll just have to drink two beers instead of one." Arlie took the paper prescription from the discharge nurse's hands and tore it half, then half again, and then three more times. "Hmm. I guess this is small enough." He turned to the nurse.

"I've seen too much trouble caused by these Mr. Happy pills."

She doesn't need to know how close you came to being addicted to them when you were shot in the back! Just get outta here to your new family!

"No problem," the nurse said, her hand opened flat to accept the shreds of prescription. "I'm sure you'll be fine in no time, although I must admit, I've never seen a person come in here covered in so many cactus needles. Dogs and cats at the vet's office, yes, but people, no. I'm sure there's an interesting story behind it, but it looks like your wife and children are here to pick you up, Arlie."

Arlie didn't correct her that Charlene wasn't his wife. Yet. She had only met him a week ago, then accepted his marriage proposal three days later. The wheels of wedding license administration didn't turn fast enough to make her his wife by Christmas, but maybe by the end of the year, she'd be Mrs. Charles Biggar.

"Daddy, Daddy," both boys called out as they raced down the hall towards him.

"Slow down, boys, and don't touch him. He still's sore, or I'm pretty sure he is," Charlene said as she hop-skipped, then speed-walked to catch up to the rambunctious pair, one her son, but both boys the biological sons of Arlie, the result of his once in a lifetime sperm donation.

The nurse paused and looked at both boys. "I can tell they're not identical twins, or at least I don't think they are, but they sure do look like you. Young men, take care of your dad and don't let him do too much, at least for another week or so. That means no roughhousing or tackle football. We don't want any of those cactus wounds to get infected now, do we?"

The nurse saw the two kindergartners' identical blank stares of confusion, so explained it another way. "You don't want him to spend Christmas day here, do you?"

"No, ma'am!"

"We'll be fine," Arlie told the suddenly fearful boys. "You know, I can't wait to get back home," he added, then winked at Charlene.

She knew he'd never been to the rental house they were all going to share. Only two days earlier, she and her son Chip had moved into the huge home that Rosa—the deceased mother of Chip's biological brother—had leased a month ago. Ever leery of her soon-to-be ex-husband—the mobster Alonzo De Luca—Rosa had stashed the large sum of cash she had purloined from Alonzo in an empty dog food bag. She also included a handwritten letter, instructions that if anything should happen to her, her new friend Charlene Barbour was to take care of her son, Carlos. Rosa's foresight had saved time in courts and spared her son from being part of the foster care system when her estranged husband and Carlos's legal father, Alonzo De Luca, had been arrested for her murder and the attempted murder of Arlie and Carlos.

Arlie gasped and bit his bottom lip as he recalled the horror. The young mother Rosa had been murdered—killed in a fiery car explosion—by the same men who nearly crippled him six months earlier in Alaska. Their brazen assault had sent him sliding down a cactus-covered mountain trail, protecting his newly-discovered son Carlos from the stepfather and uncle who had killed the boy's mother.

"I think you'll be pleasantly surprised with the changes we made," Charlene said, her voice breaking his funk. "I had a few extra bucks, so the boys and I went all out with the decorating."

"Yeah! We even got you some San..." Chip said before being cut off by shushes by his half-brother Carlos and Mom.

"You can surprise me when I get there, Chip. I'm sure it'll be the best Christmas we ever had."

Yeah, well since it's your first Christmas with them, of course it's going to be the best one, Pollyanna!

"Go open the door for him, will you, Chip?" Charlene called out, then leaned down and whispered in Arlie's ear. "Are you all right?"

"I will be when we get home." Arlie grimaced as he placed his hands on the arms of the wheelchair to sit up. "I've been on my belly for two days and in that short time, I think my muscles turned to pudding and my joints rusted dry."

"Well, I'm sure you'll be fine once you get a chance to move around. Oh, and I discovered that the master bedroom has a jetted tub! I asked the doctor and made sure it was all right for you to soak a bit. Actually, he said it would help bring out some of the smaller prickers, I mean stickers."

"Prickers may not be the correct biological name, but the way I feel about them right now, it's spot on."

"Don't worry. I'm sure the worst is behind us." Charlene stood close, letting her hand hover near his elbow to help him get the rest of the way out of the wheelchair if needed. "At least, the worst part of your physical condition."

Arlie gave a quick nod with lips pursed to stifle unexpected grunts or groans from escaping, then bent over and got into the car. He gently lowered himself into the passenger seat, then leaned back and immediately sprung forward, the tender spots of cholla and prickly pear cactus wounds raging against his body's weight.

"Here," Charlene said, and reached across him. "Let me buckle you in. Boys, get settled in. One quick stop and then it's home. Sorry, no ice cream or pizza parlor. We'll just make do with what's in the freezer or the cupboards."

"Or you can call in for a pizza," Arlie said, managing to change his grimace into a smile of recall. "I seem to remember a place nearby that has great pizza and delivers."

"Oh, yeah…" Charlene said. "That's right. You're familiar with the best pizza parlor and game room in the valley."

"Yeah, it was only a few days ago…"

Awkward, Arlie! What kind of idiot are you? Bringing up Rosa getting plastered and hitting on you the first time you ever met her…God rest her soul. Carlos is in back. He remembers going there with Charlene and Chip when his mother was still alive. Quick! Change the subject!

"I'll call ahead for delivery," Arlie said, and reached for

his phone in his shirt pocket. "Crap!" escaped his lips as his still-tender fingers fumbled the phone, dropping it in his lap.

"Here, let me," Charlene said, and retrieved it with a chuckle. "I think you'll have to play invalid for a few more days. You have me and the boys around to do your bidding. Let us take care of you." She leaned toward him and whispered, "You not only saved Carlos, you became a hero. Now they want to be just like their new daddy."

Arlie chuckled. He was still only the 'pretend' daddy to the boys, the designation applied by Charlene so the boys would be allowed to visit him in the hospital. *Looks like you're in luck! They still want you for a daddy, old man. How are you ever going to explain it to them, that they're the result of paying off a debt by jacking-off in a jar and sending the payment to your loan shark college roommate.*

Grrr!

"Are you all right, Arlie?" Charlene whispered.

Arlie's mouth twisted as he tried to figure out what to say. *Fall back on the 'I'm in pain' excuse. You milked it for six months with the police department crew after you were shot; it'll work with a Sprawl-Mart clerk and the two kids she's rearing.*

Arlie cleared his throat loudly, trying to force his negative thoughts down. "I'm sorry, Charlene. My emotions are all over the place. Part of me is the happiest person in the world, and then I move just wrong, and I'm so grumpy, I can't even stand myself. I really want to be with you and the boys, so even if I sound like a badger guarding a dead duck, ignore me. The good me is still in here, I promise."

"Didn't they give you some pain pills, or at least a prescription?"

"Oh, yeah, but I'd rather you locked me in the bathroom for a week with a case of saltine crackers for food than take those pills again. Nope, nope. Never, never." Arlie looked over and saw her concern. "It would be like giving an alcoholic the key to a liquor store with instructions to taste-test every bottle on the shelves."

"Whoa! I get it." She laughed despite herself. "I remember being in labor. I refused any pain pills. I was going to do it on my own. Well, I did. After six hours, I asked for something. The nurse said it was too close to delivery. Sorry. *Grr!* This went on every hour for the next six hours. It's a good thing I was tied down with IVs and monitors. I wanted to strangle that woman! So, yes, I know what pain is. And when he was finally born, alert and ready to take on the world, that bright red hair a warning flag to everyone to keep out of his way… Well, I was glad I hadn't had a sedative or whatever it was. Suffering through all that pain was worth being clear-headed when he finally did come out."

Arlie smiled despite himself. *What are you smiling about? You missed him being born!*

"You know, Charlene, I know I missed seeing him come into the world, and the first five and a half years, but I'll be here for both boys for the rest of their lives. And yours, too."

"That's how I feel about your sudden appearance, too. Now, I'm going to take the boys over to the sitter's place for a few hours while I get you settled in."

"Aw, Mom…" Chip whined.

"Yeah, aw, Mom," Carlos mimicked, then whispered to Chip, "What are we 'aw, Mom-ing' about?"

"Don't you want to wish Miss Ceola a merry Christmas?" Charlene asked. "Remember, you made her a present. You want to get it to her before Christmas, right?"

"Oh, yeah! Hey, Carlos, do you want to meet my sitter? Her name is Miss Ceola."

"Is a sitter like a nanny?" Carlos asked.

"Yeah, I think so. I never had a nanny. Miss Ceola watches me after school and sometimes on Saturdays if Mommy has to work. We'll have fun. Her apartments have a great big playground with a humongous slide!"

"So, I take that as a yes?" Charlene asked.

"Yes, yes," the boys chorused.

"Okay. I'll drop you off there. We'll have pizza tonight when you get home."

"Cheese, cheese!" Chip sang.

"Yes, I'll get cheese pizza. Make sure you use your manners. I'll need a couple hours to get Arlie's stuff picked up and help him get settled in."

"Is he going to live with us?" Carlos asked.

"Why, yes, I think so… That is, at least until he gets healed."

"Hopefully longer," Arlie said, and patted Charlene's leg. "'Til death do us part," he whispered so only she could hear it.

"Forever and ever," she replied, loud enough for the boys to hear, too.

It's going to be a very merry Christmas, even if you're hurting like a moose-stomped sled dog!

***

After she dropped off the boys, Charlene took a detour to Arlie's trailer park. "I thought you already picked up my goodies, not that there was much to pick up," Arlie said.

Charlene glanced down at his crotch, then giggled. "I only picked up your clothes and toiletries. I figure it's going to be a while before we get to your goodies."

Arlie laughed out loud at her unveiled *double entrendré*. "I have no idea what I'm getting into in that department, but if that's any indication, I'm glad I already asked you to marry me."

"Why? Because you think I'll always be horny?" Charlene replied, eyebrows pinched, unsure if she should be upset or not.

She started it, so don't take it as an insult. Go ahead and tell her how you really feel, jackass!

"I have no idea about what you think about me physically. I mean, look at me. I'm practically an invalid! No, I was referring to your sense of humor. I've never been married before, but I always told myself that if I was going to spend the rest of my life with a woman, she had to at least be able to match my wit, if not beat it."

Charlene glanced at his crotch again and giggled, her boisterous attitude regained after being so flattered. "Well, I guess I could beat it, but I'd rather wait for our wedding night...."

Arlie had been holding his breath, anxiously awaiting her reaction to his remark, then started to choke as he laughed and exhaled in relief at the same time.

"Are you going to be okay? I mean, I didn't mean to upset you..."

"Nope. I mean, yes, I'm okay. And no, you didn't upset me. And yes, as soon as we can, I'd like to get the marriage license procedure started so we can get married. It will probably take a few days, maybe longer, depending on the holiday break and office closures, before we can even apply. I didn't know if you wanted a fancy wedding or not. That would take a few months to plan, I'm sure. I know I don't have any family to invite, so a simple 'step before a justice of the peace' would be fine with me. Besides, all my friends are in Alaska. I wouldn't expect them to come all the way here for a wedding, but then again, I'm sure they wouldn't mind coming to Arizona for a few days of sunshine and golf in the next few weeks. Right now, Anchorage only has about four and a half hours of daylight."

Charlene put the car in park and shut off the ignition. "Hmph! My dad's in Alaska, too. Let me think about this a minute. He's the only family I have. I have a few acquaintances at Sprawl-Mart, but other than Chip's sitter, I haven't made any close friends in four years."

Thump! Thump! A heavy hand smacked the hood of the Subaru.

"Hey, there! Arlie, I didn't know you knew Charlene."

Arlie looked up and saw the smiling face of his trailer park neighbor, Dave. The good-humored senior had portrayed Santa at the elementary school where he first met Rosa and Carlos. It was only when he had volunteered to help Dave at the winter carnival that he realized his 'prankish' sperm donation years earlier had resulted in the birth of two sons by two mothers. He already knew about Charlene and Chip, the only ones he could track by sneaking into the fertility center's computer files. The other mother had disappeared off the grid soon after insemination. Evidently, she spirited off to Costa Rica, where she birthed a son, then moved to Arizona a month ago to escape her hostile and manipulative husband.

13

"Hey, Charlene. When did you meet this red-headed pup? I keep telling you, older is better!"

"Hi, Dave. I just met this wee Irish Setter recently, but we hit it off right away." She looked to Arlie. "Can I tell him?"

Arlie sat up straight and pulled his shoulders back with uninhibited pride. "You betcha!"

Charlene got out and walked around to the passenger side of the car. "Dave, it's official. Arlie is my fiancé. Sorry, but he beat you to the punch by asking me first."

Dave's eyes widened in shock, then he took in Arlie's swollen cactus-needle punctured face. "You're kidding me…"

Arlie and Charlene shook their heads at the same rate, looking like synchronized bobble-head dolls.

"Really? You move fast, Arlie!"

"Well, when it's the right thing to do, and you know it here," Arlie said, and gently patted the seatbelt crossing his heart. "There's no reason to wait. Now, that being said, I've had a bit of a kerfuffle and am limited in my ability to help with much of anything. The other day, I put together a bike for Chip's Christmas present. Would you help Charlene load it into the back of the station wagon?"

Dave turned to Charlene. "Your Chip? The one in my

Davey's kindergarten class?"

"Our Chip," Arlie answered. "He's mine, too."

"Now, I'm confused, Arlie. If you allow me a moment before I help your lovely fiancée load up the bike." Dave held onto the door handle and squatted down next to Arlie. "I thought it was some other boy you saved from the bad guys the other day. I'm sure I would have recognized Chip's name. The last name was Smith or Jones or something common like that."

Arlie shifted slightly in the passenger seat in order to see Dave better, but also to have time to think about what he had just heard. "How did you know about me and young Carlos Smith?"

"Shoot! It was all over the news on TV and in the newspapers. Of course, that meant it was also on the internet. 'Hero tumbles through cactus to save child from mobsters.' Or maybe they said villains or bad guys, I can't remember. I did save the newspaper article for you, though."

Arlie chuckled. "Maybe later. Right now, I just want to get home. Charlene dropped the boys off at the sitter so we could get these last few gifts set up for Christmas."

"Boys? What? Did you just pop another one out

overnight, Charlene?"

"Not quite that fast. I don't know if it was in the same article, but it's highly suspected that those bad guys killed the mother of young Carlos Smith just before they came after him. As you already read and heard, Arlie stopped them.

"When all the paperwork was done at the sheriff's office, I just up and took Carlos with me. The two boys looked so much alike, the authorities didn't so much as frown when I headed out the door with him. Maybe they thought the two were cousins and I was his aunt. Actually, since his legal father was the one who tried to shoot Carlos and they had him in custody, they would have had to scramble to find a foster family for him. Plus, they could tell the three of us were comfortable with each other. Don't ask, don't tell worked for everybody this time.

"As it turned out, Rosa didn't trust her husband and had left a note giving me custody of him. It wasn't witnessed, and it wasn't until after we had left the sheriff's station that we found the note. I still haven't had to show it to anyone. Hmmm. Maybe you can witness it for me…"

"Charlene, I know you're a wonderful woman, but I don't know who this other mother was… Whoa! Wait! You said

Rosa? She's the new lady whose son looks like Chip's twin, right?"

"She was. The men who shot Arlie and tried to kill Carlos killed her. Or that's what the cops suspect."

"They shot Arlie?" Dave put his hand on his forehead. "It can't be the sun getting to me because it's barely warm today. Yes, I'll sign and witness your document and back date it if it will help you keep the boy safe, but you got shot, Arlie? I thought it was just the cactus ride you suffered through."

"Yes, I got shot, but it didn't hurt me. I have you to thank for not getting another bullet in the back. This one put a hole in my already cactus-ripped and torn shirt, then hit the stereo magnet in that modified back brace your created for me. I'll be forever grateful. By the way, that little two-inch magnet was so powerful that over the two days I wore the belt/back brace, it sucked that six-month old bullet away from my spine. It pulled it out so far that the doctor removing the cactus stickers could see it just under my skin. He just made a small incision and grabbed it with tweezers. Or forceps. Or whatever it is he used."

"Two bullets?" Dave asked. "You already had a bullet in

your back and that's why you were hurting so bad?"

"Yeah. Line of duty injury. I'm an Anchorage cop."

"Oh…"

Arlie's head slumped to one side as he shut his eyes. "I'm wearing out fast, Dave. If it's not too much to ask, can you go ahead and help Charlene wrangle Carlos and Chip's presents into the car?"

"I'm on it!" Dave answered, then turned and whispered to Charlene, "He's a cop?"

"Yup, a detective. He's smart *and* cute!"

Dave got the bike while Charlene opened the back of the car and pushed the rear seats down, making room for Chip's Christmas present, the shiny Stingray bicycle Arlie had put together, and the look alike banana seat that was Carlos's present for the bike his mother had bought for him just weeks earlier.

"You did a great job putting the bike together, Arlie," Charlene said after she got back in the car. "But I noticed that when you put the fancy banana seat on it, you didn't use the bag of hardware that came with it, or at least all the pieces." She held up the torn bag of bolts and washers, nearly full. "I've never put a bike seat on, but if I was a gambling person,

I'd bet this bag was short one three-inch bolt."

"Oh, Lord… I knew I was tired when I got to that point in assembly. I forgot the new seat came with its own hardware. I'm sure I opened it, but then it got shuffled under something and I went ahead and reused the hardware for the original seat. That leftover bolt I stuffed in my pocket saved Carlos's life and cost that sorry S.O.B. his hearing…"

"Yeah, well how many men would be clever or brave enough to attack an armed man using only a bolt?"

Arlie chucked. "Only one guarding the life of someone dear to him. Just make sure you check over the bike before Chip tries it out. I sat on it and it felt sturdy, but it was late…"

Charlene looked over, waiting for the rest of the story, but Arlie had fallen asleep in mid-sentence. Tuckered out, he looked just like Chip, his fist stuffed under his chin. Smiling.

***

Charlene pulled into the garage of the big rental house, unloaded the bike and rolled it into the laundry room, parked it next to Carlos's identical ride, grabbed the gifts, then returned to the car.

She looked at the man who she had agreed to marry on a whim and felt a twinge of guilt. Why had she said yes? Was it the emotional high of his saving a young boy's life, of being scared for her own life, then relief when the shootout had a happy ending?

"Not hardly," she whispered.

It's not the events, but the man behind the actions. Arlie's uninhibited, fearless resolve is spectacular. And his honesty: he's never lied to me, even though he could have done so early on so I wouldn't question him further. He hasn't known me long enough to tell his whole story, of why he tracked me down as the mother of his biological son, but I'm sure he'll get there. Of course, it doesn't hurt to fall for a guy who's about my age and who has a nice body. So far, no bad habits, either: no drinking, smoking, cursing—even under dire circumstances. He didn't take advantage of Rosa when she was drunk and hanging all over him. And even though he was in extreme pain, he kept away from popping pills. Plus, Arlie looks just like Chip. His son. My son. OUR son.

Charlene leaned close to his face, ready to kiss him, then changed her mind and pulled back, this time taking in all his facial features. His eyelashes were the same dark reddish brown as Chip's, and he had the same attached earlobes, too. She had already noticed that both had dark coffee-brown eyes, and although Arlie's hair was a darker red color, it might be because he was both older and hadn't been in the Arizona sun for five years like Chip.

"Where will you and I be in five years?" she whispered.

"Hopefully, inside, or at least, out of the car," Arlie whispered back.

Charlene jerked away in surprise, smacking the top of her head on the inside of the car door frame. "I thought you were asleep!"

"I was. I thought I was dreaming that you were close to me, wanting to get closer. I could even smell you, and then I heard you breathing. I realized that this was much better than a dream. You were real. And real close." Arlie held up his hand and touched the air in front of her, as if she was an apparition he was afraid to disturb lest she vanish.

Charlene touched the dent in the top of her head and winced. "Yeah, well I'm real, all right. I almost got closer, too, then realized that I wouldn't like it if you *took* our first kiss rather than shared it. At least, with both of us wide awake. Come on, let me help you get inside. We only have an hour or so before I'm supposed to pick up the boys."

She reached across to unbuckle Arlie, then stood back

as the seatbelt retracted. "The boys. That sounds strange, as in unfamiliar, but it also sounds right."

"I disagree."

Charlene frowned, but didn't say anything, her eyes intent on his face. There had to be more to his comment.

"I think 'our boys' sounds better."

A stifled laugh escaped as Charlene held up her hand, palm out. "I'll have to give you an air high five for now. Let's get you upstairs to the bath!"

Arlie lifted his arm and sniffed. "Ew! I haven't had a bath in two days."

"Three days, but don't worry about it. I gave you a sponge bath while you were out. You were getting a little ripe there..."

"Can we continue this conversation upstairs? I need to concentrate..." Arlie straightened up. "Umph!"

"Here, let me get the door knobs. The master bedroom and bath are at the top of the stairs and to the right. Can you make it, or do you want me to help?"

Arlie looked through the doorway into the huge house. "It doesn't look this big from the street view..."

"Come on. You can take in the sights later. I'm sure the

boys—er, our boys—will be happy to give you a guided tour when they come back." Charlene held up the plastic hospital bag that held his belongings. "And if you don't mind, I'm going to toss these old clothes. I thought you might want to go through the pockets first. You can supervise me while I do it because you won't be able to use those fingers for much of anything for a few days."

Arlie sniffed, then winked. "I'll let you know if I need help blowing my nose then…"

Charlene laughed. "You forget. I'm a mom. I've wiped more than runny noses. Oh, and here we are."

"Wow! I made it all the way up without stopping or whining. God, I sound pathetic. Getting excited about climbing a set of carpet-covered stairs."

"Yeah, well, I distracted you on purpose; that's another mommy trick. Now, don't take offense at this, but I'm going to insist that I'm in charge of everything you do, at least until tomorrow morning. The doctor said to take it easy, just in case you're still suffering from some side effects."

"Side effects from cactus thorns?" Arlie asked. "And earlier you said I was out three days, not two…"

Charlene turned on the tub faucet and dumped in the

Epsom salts and baking soda mix she had concocted earlier. She checked the temperature and swirled the salty blend through the rapidly filling tub. "I didn't think you remembered it. I'll tell you about it, but first, let me help you out of your clothes. Right arm first…"

As he stood beside her, eyes closed, Arlie followed her prompts, letting her remove his shirt, then unbutton and unzip his pants. When they first spoke of her helping him with a bath, he had been afraid he'd be embarrassed by a raging erection. But now that he was totally stunned about a day being sucked out of his life without him knowing about it, it looked like he'd have the opposite problem: fear induced, shrinky-dick syndrome. Shoot, if that happened, she might never want to bed him!

"Look at me, Arlie," she said, breaking his trance of fear and insecurity.

He opened his eyes and saw he had unconsciously been responding to her disrobing prompts, and all he had on now were red and green plaid boxers. "What the…?"

"I wasn't the one who undressed you in the hospital, and your clothes were in a plastic bag and too prickly to touch much less look through without gloves, so I didn't know if you were a boxers or briefs kind of guy. Maybe I guessed wrong, I don't know. Actually, I let Chip and Carlos pick these out for you, so maybe we all guessed wrong. I don't want you to get in the tub without help. So, shorts on or off?"

"Leave them on for now," he replied, his voice low and despondent.

"Arlie," Charlene stood close, close enough to smell the fear on him and see the goosebumps rise on his chest. "I'm not trying to keep anything from you, but obviously, you don't remember what happened. They brought you to the hospital after the row at Lost Dutchman Park…"

"Yeah, and I helped save Carlos from his legal father, Alonzo De Luca," Arlie spat over his shoulder and away from Charlene, "by tumbling down a cactus-covered hill with the boy in my arms, then stabbing the old man in the ear with the leftover part from Chip's bicycle. The cops took away both De Luca brothers, I went to the ER and they sedated me to pull out all the cactus thorns—or most of them. The doc also removed that old bullet from when Alonzo," Arlie gave another dry, exaggerated spit over his shoulder, "shot me in the back six months ago in Alaska."

Arlie stepped into the water and his anger lessened, his

voice and body posture relaxed. "I remember waking up, lying on my belly, the boys telling me that what they wanted for Christmas was for me to be their daddy, and you." He sighed in contentment and looked to his fiancée dressed in an oversized Arizona Cardinals tee-shirt. "I was wide awake when I asked you to be my wife…"

He settled into the tub, his eyes still focused on her. The warm, silky-smooth water, and the buoyancy of near weightlessness removed the pressure of the subcutaneous tiny cactus stickers that still plagued him. "The memory of your face when you said yes to my lackluster but sincere proposal will be my happiest memory ever, no doubt about that."

"Unless we make a few other great ones." Charlene pushed the power button on the jacuzzi jets.

"Ahh…" Arlie paused to enjoy the bubbly sensation. "Yes, I'm sure we'll make many more happy memories, but this will always be my favorite because it was my first one with you and the boys." Arlie's grin faded into a scowl as his detective persona took over. "So, after my proposal and your acceptance, we talked a bit more, then you took the boys home, right?"

"Yes, I took *our* boys home. Here, to our first home together. Carlos had enough clothes for Chip and Rosa's clothes fit me, so we were set. She even had duplicates and triplicates of toiletries, still in the wrappers. The next morning—after I called in and quit my job—I called Miss Ceola and asked her to watch Chip and his almost twin for the day while I took care of their father. She agreed, so there I was at the hospital, the anxious yet excited fiancée, ready to mother hen my man.

"I watched you wake up, refuse pain pills, accept sips of juice and water from me, then drift off to sleep again. The nurses said sleeping on and off for a day was normal after being under general anesthesia. I decided to go downstairs to the cafeteria and grab some real food. I brought it back and there was someone in the room, trying to give you an injection. You were out of it, arms flailing in refusal, but he was insistent. I knew you didn't want any more pain killers, so I told him to back off. I literally had to get between the two of you to keep him from giving you that shot.

"And then I noticed it: no name tag. He was wearing a scrubs top, but was in skinny jeans and designer cross trainers."

Arlie held up one finger, asking her to pause a moment, then slipped under the water, covering his face completely. He held his breath as long as he could, then blew out all his air, and resurfaced. "God, that feels good," he said. "I wish I had a snorkel… I'm sorry. I just had to do that. Now, don't tell me: the guy had black hair, a big mustache, and eyes the color of road tar."

"Were you awake?"

"No, I don't think so. It was the skinny jeans and fancy footwear description. The De Luca brothers—and cousins, too, I suspect—wear them almost as a bad guys' uniform. Sorry I interrupted. What happened next? I mean, I know I survived, but I still lost a day."

"I kneed him in the nuts," Charlene said bluntly, then started chuckling. "It startled him so much, he threw the syringe up in the air. I grabbed the bed pan—which you had not used—and captured it without getting stuck. He was still bent over, cussing me out, when I stepped forward and kneed him again, this time, catching him in the nose. 'You'd better leave right now, sucka!' I hollered."

"Yeah? And then what?"

"He split. I started to pick up the syringe, then realized it

28

probably had his fingerprints on it. I didn't remember him wearing gloves—bad nurse—so I grabbed a few paper towels, wrapped it up, and stashed it in my purse. I didn't think he'd injected you, but I wanted it in case you were going to press charges or whatever. I'm not a cop, but I do know my way around a courtroom."

"Yeah, I know," Arlie said, then grimaced. *Now you've done it, dummy! You let her know you know about her past!* "So, where is it now? I'd like to get it sent off to Abby as soon as possible."

Arlie sat up and leaned forward, as if he was going to get out of the tub, then said, "Dang! I feel like I have a hangover. The nurse told me it was one of the aftereffects of general anesthesia, but it should have been gone by now."

"I kinda, sorta beat you to the punch with Abby. I already sent it to her."

"How?"

"Express Mail. The guy at the post office said she'd have it by Christmas Day."

"I mean, how did you know where to send it?"

"Oh, she and I talked for a while earlier. You know, girly stuff."

"Abby? Talking girly stuff? What kind of girly stuff?"

"Oh, what color wedding dress was I going to wear, long or short, that kind of girly stuff."

"You called her? And told her about the wedding?"

"No. Well, kinda, and yes. The first time we talked was after she had sent the cops to the park. You know, after the sheriffs found Rosa murdered and you two talked on the phone on top of the trail at Lost Dutchman Park? Of course, when Abby called back, she didn't know you had just done a few cactus cartwheels and were in an ambulance on the way to the hospital. Since I had your phone with me and recognized the *zippidee doo dah* ring tone as hers, I answered it. I filled her in on what had happened, and then we swapped numbers. Actually—and I thought this was rather strange at the time—she made me promise to call her if you asked me to marry you. So, I promised, then I did."

"That's a strange way to start a friendship, but okay. So, after the attack by the phony nurse, you called her, and she gave you instructions on how and where to ship the syringe?"

"Ten-four, darling. She said she'd even come in on Christmas Day to check it out. So, since it's still in the postal system and there's nothing we can do about it now,"

Charlene cupped water in her hands and poured it down the back of his neck, "How about a little just you and me time?"

"I'll let you do that as long as the water stays warm…"

"If that was our only limitation, we'd never get out of here. See," Charlene pointed to the button on the edge of the tub, then pushed it. "This has a build-in heater."

"You do realize that this tub is big enough for two, right?" Arlie asked, then scooted toward the side to make room for Charlene.

"And I did say I'd take care of you… Here, let me take off some of these clothes."

Arlie watched as she stood up and pulled the oversized tee shirt off over her head, revealing a sexy demi bra and short, skimpy athletic shorts. "As I said, Rosa and I were about the same size. I don't think I've ever owned a bra this fancy, though…"

"How long until you have to pick up Chip and Carlos?" Arlie asked, the edges of his grin practically tickling his earlobes.

"I'm sure it will be too soon," she said and stepped in the tub. She reached behind her and grabbed a washcloth, then sat down all the way. "Oh, my. This does feel good!" then leaned back and slipped underwater, copying Arlie's submerged soaking.

"God, you're beautiful," Arlie said when she came up for air. "I just said that out loud, didn't I?"

"Either that or the water in my ears is causing hallucinations. Actually, despite your battle on the cholla and prickly pear hillside, you're pretty good looking, too." Charlene glanced down at his chest, then brought up the dripping wet washcloth. "Nice broad shoulders, too. Now I know where Chip gets them."

She stroked her fingertips under his collarbone, felt a bump, then gently swiped the washcloth over it. She felt again, this time holding up a tiny bit of cactus. "It looks like this is going to take a while. We might not be able to get it done before our time's up."

"Why are you being so wonderful to me? I mean, I'm grateful, and part of me feels so fantastic," Arlie said, then crossed his hands over the burgeoning gap in his boxer shorts, a broad mischievous smile covering his face. He chuckled, then a frown sneaked in and he let out with a disgruntled sigh, "But part of me is guilt-ridden..."

Pbbt! "You gave me a son without the complication of a

husband." She shook her head. "I think that came out wrong..."

"All you wanted at the time was a child, right?" Arlie suggested, a sliver of a smile returning to his face. "And now, six years later, you're ready for the husband part?"

Charlene turned sideways and came in close, as if to kiss him. "Such a perfect explanation. I wish I could kiss you without hurting you."

"You can..."

"But your lips are still tender, right?"

"I'm still able to eat. How about a little food for my soul?"

Her lips barely touched his as she leaned across him. "My soul's been starved for years..."

"Then let's feed each other..."

Chapter 2
Why do you want to marry me?

Random relationship facts: If you want your marriage to have a higher success rate, wait until you're older to commit! Couples who appreciate each other and share the same interests are more likely to stay together. Also, the happiest marriages are between best friends!

Brrrnng! Brrrnng! Brrrnng!

Arlie pulled away from the lingering kiss. "What was that?" he mumbled, curious about the noise, but reluctant to give up even a moment of tactile time with Charlene.

"Um, I set the timer on the microwave in case we got carried away. It may not feel like it, but we've been up here for an hour." She sat up straight and groaned at the loss of physical contact. "I'm sure glad there's more where that came from."

"I'm all yours, darling," Arlie cooed, then shifted his back and shoulders, rocking back and forth until he was sitting up straight.

"I need to go get the boys." Charlene held up her hand

and inspected both sides. "I guess it's time, anyway. The water may still be warm, but that didn't stop me from getting all pruney. How are you doing?"

Arlie mirrored her hand-twisting examination. "Actually, not too bad. While you're gone, I think I'll do a bit more washcloth thorn-removal. I don't know why the hospital didn't suggest it. I used to wash dishes by hand whenever I got a sliver in my finger, whether the dishes were dirty or not."

"Do you think you'll be able to get out of the tub without my help?"

Arlie glanced down, then reached across his lap, tucking the edges of his boxers over the part of him that had caused the gap. "I'll be fine. I think I'll stay in here for a while longer." He reached over and turned off the heater, "at least until the water cools down."

***

Charlene pulled up to the house after the quick round trip. The boys had fallen asleep on the ride back from Miss Ceola's and were slumped over each other. "Hey, guys," she whispered. When they didn't respond, she tried again, a little louder. "Hey, guys! It's Christmas Eve. Why don't you grab the treats Miss Ceola baked for us and come in the house?

The pizza should be here pretty quick, too."

Chip and Carlos sat up, looked at each other and grinned as they shared the same thought. "Is Arlie—I mean Daddy—still here?" Chip asked.

"Yeah, is he still our daddy?" Carlos added.

"Absolutely. Forever and ever. I need to go upstairs and make sure he didn't fall asleep in the tub. Come inside and arrange your gifts in order of which ones you want to open first."

"Can we open our presents tonight?" Chip asked.

"Yeah, can we?" Carlos added.

"If we open them tonight, what are you going to do on Christmas morning?" Charlene asked, and picked up one of Chip's gifts and swung it in front of his face by the ribbon.

"Play with all the presents!"

"Well, let me go get your dad and ask him what he thinks," she said. "Stay down here by the tree. I'll be back in a minute."

***

Arlie leaned over the edge of the tub and tried to figure out the safest and least messy way to get out.

"Here, let me help you," Charlene said when she walked

in and saw his dilemma. "But I want to take off some of these clothes first, so I don't get soaked."

"If you take off that tee shirt, I don't think I'll ever let you leave. It was hard enough being close to you with that splash of red lace barely containing your breasts. And those gray athletic shorts were as plain as a trash bag, but they sure enhanced what came out of them! No need for you to get wet. Just come stand here and steady me in case my legs give out. They feel like soggy noodles."

"I'm glad you were finally able to relax, but other than that, how do you feel?"

Arlie pushed himself up, holding onto to Charlene's arm. "I feel fantastic!" He stood up straight, then twisted his shoulders while still grasping his physical and emotional support. He squeezed her forearm before letting go, saying, 'thanks' wordlessly for all the help she'd given him. "Let me get out of these soggy shorts and I'll be right down to join you and the boys."

Ding dong! Ding dong!

"Pizza?" Arlie asked, just as Charlene said, "Pizza!"

"You're sure you can make it by yourself?"

"If I can't, I'll call."

"I'm stuffed!" Charlene said, and pushed away her plate.

"Not me," Arlie said, and grabbed the half-eaten piece she had set down. "How about you two? Did you eat enough to last you until breakfast?"

"Yeah, yeah!" the boys chorused as they bounced up and down in their chairs. "Can we open our presents when you're done?"

Arlie nodded as he took a bite out of the pizza slice, then set it back on Charlene's plate. "I guess I'm stuffed, too." He sat up tall, and frowned as he looked from one son to the other. "There's a lot of gifts under that tree. Do you think you deserve all those presents?"

"Yes, sir," Carlos said, suddenly insecure.

"Uh huh, I mean, yes, sir," Chip added, then reached over and held Carlos's hand. "We've both been real good, all year long. Well, at least we have been since we've been brothers. I don't know about him when he lived in Coca Cola, but I know he's been good since he came to school with me."

"And can either one of you tell me why we should wait until tomorrow and not open them right now?"

"Nuh uh," Chip exclaimed, jumping up and down. "I think

we should open them now! Then we'll sleep good tonight and won't wake up when Santa comes. Mommy always let me open one present early, just so I'd sleep better, but we have so many..."

"Yeah, we'll sleep real good tonight if we get to open all of them now," Carlos added, his hands clutched together under his chin, more sedate than his brother in actions, but his eyes just as sparkling with anticipation.

"They do have a point," Charlene said. "And it would be nice not to worry about them waking up in the middle of the night to see Santa. These should tide them over."

"How did you get so many presents in such a short time? I didn't think you had that much time for shopping with spending time with me at the hospital and taking care of the boys."

"It wasn't me. I bought a gift or two for all of you, but Rosa had 'pre-shopped' and had wrapped a whole roomful of gifts. Well, at least the walk-in closet in the second bedroom was stacked with them. I have no idea what they're getting, either. Carlos and Chip spent one night shaking boxes, then splitting them up on either side of the Christmas tree." Charlene shook her head. "For being so entitled and rich, he sure is a sweet and generous child."

"Daddy, do you want to open one first?" Chip asked. "Carlos and I picked it out just for you."

Arlie's eyes misted up unexpectedly. He looked at Charlene before answering, taking the time to wipe away the tears before they fell. *Go ahead and let her see how great you feel, dummy! Women like a gentle, caring man. She probably already knows what a big deal this is for you: your first Christmas gift from your sons.*

"Yes, sons, I'd be honored to open the first present, especially if you picked it out yourselves."

"I'll take care of the dishes later," Charlene said, stacking the paper plates on top of each other, then wadding up the soiled napkins and adding them to the pile. "Let's go to the tree, men!"

While Charlene helped Arlie arrange throw pillows behind his back, Chip and Carlos dug through the mounds of colorfully wrapped boxes to find the one Arlie could tell they had wrapped themselves. At first, Chip clutched the box close to his chest, then seeing the frown on Carlos's face, held it out so they could carry it together across the room to the first caring father either of them had ever had.

The unexpected show of brotherly love brought another unbidden tear to Arlie's face. He wiped it from his cheek with the shoulder of his tee shirt, then said, "It's beautiful, sons." Turning it over in his hands, he noted that they had probably used a whole roll of tape in securing the action hero-themed holiday paper to the breadbox-sized container.

"We wanted to make sure you didn't peek inside and see what it was," Chip explained.

"May I open it now?" Arlie asked, then held the box to his ear and shook it.

"Guess what it is," Carlos said, giddy at the opportunity to interact with a kind man, not one who would fly into a rage at a misspoken word or an unchoreographed action.

"Is it a hippopotamus?"

"No!" the boys chorused.

"My two front teeth?" Arlie teased, then ran his tongue over his teeth and added, "I guess not. I still have them. Hmm. What can it be? May I look now?"

"Yeah, yeah! Look now!"

"Here," Charlene said, and held out the scissors, then brought them back. "Or do you want me to do it?"

Arlie looked at the package, his swollen hands, and the

scissors that were sure to hurt his tender, cactus-pricked thumb and fingers. "Only if I can supervise. Here, cut here first."

"One voice-activated gift box opener, at your service." Charlene made the first cut, then waited for Arlie to point to the next spot.

The boys giggled at the merriment created by their parents adapting to Dad's physical limitations. Soon, Arlie and Charlene were laughing, too. "Are you sure you don't want me to cut here first?" Mom asked.

"No, no, get this side next," Arlie would answer, just to be contrary.

When the box was finally unwrapped, Charlene stuck her fingers between the top and bottom of the Christmas print box. "Now?" she asked.

Arlie inhaled, savoring the moment, then leaned forward and sniffed next to her hands. "I want to guess again." He inhaled again, this time confirming what he suspected. Before he could even think to continue their silly gift-guessing game, he said, "A baseball mitt!"

Charlene pulled open the box. "Ta da!" she exclaimed.

"Oh! Three mitts and a baseball!" Arlie amended, then

the tears fell, uninhibited by the restraint men were traditionally supposed to keep imprisoned inside.

The boys, still standing in front of him from the impromptu package reveal game, stared at him, eyes wide in worry. He pulled them close. "These are tears of joy. When you're older and have children of your own, you'll know how wonderful it is to be able to play that first game of catch. Thanks, guys. This is the perfect gift."

"Mommy said we should get gloves for us, too, and put them in the box at the same time," Chip said. "That way you'd know we wanted to play catch, too. I think we'll have to wait until later when your hands are healed, but she said you'd like the mitts and ball, no matter when you got them. She was right, huh?"

Arlie wiped his nose with the Santa-adorned paper napkin Charlene handed him, then looked over at her as she settled onto the floor in front of the tree. "Yes, your mother is usually right. Remember that. And if she's not, then it just means either you didn't understand her, or she didn't have all the information to make a good decision."

"Wow!" she said, her face even brighter with happiness. "I didn't know you were that wonderful. I'm glad I got you to propose when I did!"

"Yes, my sweet, I'm not sure if I chased you until you caught me or if it was the other way around. Either way, we're like hook and loop tape, Velcro that will stick together no matter which side you start with."

"Mommy, are you and Daddy going to get all mushy or can we open our presents now?" Chip asked.

Carlos elbowed his brother. "It's okay if they get all mushy. It's better than fighting. Besides, the presents are still here and I'm not tired at all!"

"All right, all right," Arlie said, then nodded to Charlene. "Your mother will supervise while I kick back and watch. Merry Christmas, everyone!"

The boys took turns opening presents, saving favorites in one pile, others that they weren't too attached to in another one, 'the share with others' pile.

Charlene brought out a Christmas-themed bag for Arlie, stuffed with tissue paper. "I wrapped this one so you could open it without help," she said, and set it in his lap.

"But I didn't..."

"If you're going to say, 'I didn't get a chance to buy you something,' please don't. What you've given me money can't buy: the best Christmas Eve I've ever had."

Arlie caught her eye, then glanced at Chip, then looked at her again.

"Yeah, well, more than a couple bucks changed hands with the fertility center on that gift…"

"The next one will be totally on me," Arlie whispered as she came close, then he nibbled her ear.

Charlene failed to contain her squeal. "When did you say we could get married?"

Arlie looked at the imaginary watch on his wrist. "As soon as the justice of the peace comes in. Now, let me see what you got me." He tugged at the tissue paper, pulled the works out of the bag, and found the colorful fabric. "Santa shorts?" he asked.

"They're sleep shorts. Or boxers. Or swim shorts, I suppose. The boys wanted to get them. I figured they'd work until you could do your own shopping."

Chip stood astride the new Stingray bicycle Arlie had put together the week before. "Mommy, when can we ride our bikes?"

"Here, let me hold on to the back of the seat while you try pedaling around the dining room. I'm not sure how quickly you'll get your balance. We may have to get training wheels for this." Charlene grasped the top of the curved bar at the back of the banana seat with one hand and the fancy plastic handlebar grip with the other, then led him in a loop around the kitchen island. "Wow! You got this, dude!" she said, amazed at how easy it was.

"Yeah, Miss Ceola's oldest son helped me learn. He said I needed to be prepared in case Santa got me a bike for Christmas."

"Look at me!" Carlos said.

"Great balance, buddy," Arlie said, then jumped up from the couch to plant himself in front of Carlos before he rolled into the oversized Christmas tree. "But I think you're going to have to work on your braking skills. We can do that tomorrow. Let's put the bikes in the garage for now."

"Yes, guys. It's brush your teeth and go to bed time." Charlene looked up at the clock. "It's 9:30! It's way past brush your teeth time!"

***

"I can't believe they wanted to stay up to thank Santa for sneaking in early to give them their presents. I know Chip got his good manners from you, but from what Carlos has mentioned about his past, he was pretty much brought up by nannies or governesses."

"Yeah, well, he had at least one good strong parental figure along the way. He's pretty well adjusted," Charlene ran her fingers through Arlie's wavy locks. "Changing the subject now," she said, "How come a cop has such long hair?"

"I'm an undercover detective. I guess I could have taken the time to get a traditional haircut when I was given a desk job, but I kept expecting to get over being a near cripple." Arlie flipped the hair off his forehead in a rakish manner. "But I think I look rather dashing like this, don't you?"

Charlene kissed the bared brow, then kept giving him gentle, teasing pecks until she reached his mouth. Rather than give in to the full kiss she was certain he was expecting, she pulled away. "So, what you're saying is you had faith that you'd get better, correct?"

"Hmm. I never thought about it like that, but I guess that's right. I know I hoped I would get better, but if I hadn't had faith, I would have been in the barber's chair, getting a fresh buzz cut on the first of every month."

Just as Charlene bent down to finish what she had started, she heard one of the boys whisper harshly, "Shush, or Mommy will hear us."

"To be continued," Arlie mumbled into her hair as she sat up.

"Promise?"

"As sure as the sun will rise tomorrow," he answered.

"Why are you boys awake? Didn't we agree that you could open the presents early if you went to bed on time and *stayed* there?" Charlene asked, hands on hips in her no-nonsense stance.

Chip elbowed Carlos and said, "Give it to her. She can give it to him."

Carlos squirmed in place, rolling his shoulders like he was wearing a shirt that was two sizes too small. "We wrote a letter to Santa..."

"He wrote the words, but I helped him know what to say," Chip interrupted. "Go ahead. You can read it to her, then maybe she'll let us put out milk and cookies, just in case he does come back."

Carlos glanced up, then cast his eyes back down and reached out to give Charlene the letter scripted with what appeared to be an eyebrow pencil.

Charlene read the note aloud, "Dear Santa. Thank you

for the toys and stuff. We want you to have cookies and milk and carrots for your rain dear. Love brothers Carlos and Chip."

Arlie exhaled loudly, trying to figure out what to say about the note. Charlene saw his speechless expression and mouthed, 'I got this.'

"So, boys, you weren't trying to wait up for Santa, then?"

Carlos shook his head as Chip shrugged his shoulder. Carlos saw what he had done, then elbowed him, causing Chip to shake his head reluctantly.

"I have milk and a box of cookies, but we don't have any carrots. I do have some apples, though. Do you think I can just write at the bottom of your note and tell Santa the reindeer will get bright red, juicy apples instead of carrots?"

Carlos and Chip looked at each other, wide-eyed with excitement, then grasped each other's hands and jumped up and down. "Yeah, yeah!"

"All right, then. Go back to bed and I'll let Santa know the cookies and milk are for him and the apples are for Rudolph and his friends. You can play with your toys in the morning, then ride your bikes after it gets warmer. But we all need our sleep, right?"

"Yes, Mommy. I love you. I love you, too, Daddy," Chip said, then giggled behind his hand.

"Me, too," Carlos said, then grabbed Chip's hand and said. "Let's go to sleep so morning will get here faster!"

"Arlie," Charlene said after the boys had settled back into their beds. "I think I'd better sleep on the couch tonight. I hope you don't mind, but…"

"Not trying to put words in your mouth, but it's okay if there are several reasons you want to be on the couch tonight. There's nothing for the boys to get into, but I think I'd just frustrate myself if you were sleeping next to me. Believe me, the desire is there, and I could probably…"

"No second guessing on either part. We'll get there, but something tells me that tonight shouldn't be the night."

Chapter 3
Smoke alarms save lives

From the reporting period of 2007 to 2011, the death rate from home fires that had at least one functioning smoke alarm was 0.61deaths per 100 fires compared to 0.95 deaths per 100 for homes without a smoke alarm. This translates to a 36% lower fatality rate and a lot of lives saved for homes with functional smoke alarms!

Cough! Cough!

"What the…" Arlie grabbed the moist washcloth from the nightstand and put it over his mouth, pulled on his Santa boxers, and raced downstairs, steadying himself on the railing as he stumbled through the smoky haze in haste.

"Fire! Fire!" he shouted, then gagged and put the washcloth over his mouth again.

Thick gray clouds swirled above the living room, the ceiling fan sucking them up to the second floor, leaving the ground floor significantly less smoky.

Charlene sat up from her Santa sentinel post on the couch and asked, "Wait, what?" then she started coughing, too.

"Where are the boys?" he asked, pulling her to her feet. "Which room? I don't know my way around this place."

Charlene brought the neckline of her nightshirt up to cover her mouth. Trying not to inhale, she mumbled, "This way," and clutched Arlie's hand, leading him down the hall. "In here," she said, and shoved open the bedroom door that had been left ajar for the fear-of-the-dark Carlos.

"I'll grab one and you get the other, but you take the lead," Arlie said, throwing the covers off one boy. "Get up, son."

"Is Santa here?" Chip mumbled, still half-asleep.

"Let's go see," Arlie said, and hoisted the disoriented child over his shoulder.

Carlos, bright-eyed with terror, rocketed out of bed and clutched Charlene close, his head shaking back and forth in disbelief. "This way," Charlene said, and turned right, Arlie's hand light on her shoulder.

The intense but level-headed mother grabbed the front door handle with one hand, then let go of Carlos's hand and tried a two-hand approach when it wouldn't open.

"Let me try," Arlie said, and pulled on it with his one free hand. "Crap!"

He set Chip down. "Stay put," he said, then yanked on the door with both hands, ignoring the pain, one foot braced against the door jam. He twisted the dead bolt and handle, back and forth then back again to no avail. "I think it's jammed. Hold on. I have an idea."

Arlie grabbed one of the tall bistro chairs from the breakfast nook. "Lean forward and cover your heads!" he screamed, the roar of the flames in the garage now punctuated with pops and booms from aerosol cans exploding. He threw the metal-framed chair through the plate glass picture window, then ducked, covering his face with his inner elbow.

Charlene grabbed the mattress from the futon while Arlie used the coffee table to break out and sweep away the larger shards from the window frame. "Let me help," he said. The two parents set the mattress over the broken glass, providing a padded bridge up to and over the window opening. "You first, then I'll hand you the boys."

The barefoot parents shuttled the boys out, then Arlie said, "Go over to the light pole and stay put, all of you." He turned to go back inside. "I'll be right back."

Charlene grabbed his wrist. "Oh, no you don't!" She

jerked him towards her, no argument or discussion allowed. "There's nothing on this earth that's worth you going back in."

Arlie started to pull away, then realized she was correct. "You're right. Come on."

Two by two, the four held hands as they dashed over the pebbly asphalt to the halogen light pole 50 yards away. Sirens blared in the background, the urgent whines accompanied by the sporadic popping and crackling of the frame-built stucco house, now half-engulfed in orange and yellow sheets of flames, illuminating the moonless night in a surreal yet beautiful glow.

"I'm cold, Mommy," Chip said, and snuggled close.

"Me, too," Carlos said, and wrapped his arms around Charlene's other side, clasping Chip's wrists to secure his hold on his new mother.

Arlie moved up to Charlene's back, then gathered all three of them in a broad, protective hug. He stifled a cough, then whispered in her ear, "I can't believe I almost went in there for my pearl-handled revolver and phone..."

She turned to him, "I'll bet they drill keeping your weapon with you at all times in training, though, right?"

He coughed and chuckled at the same time. "Actually, it

was a gift from an old friend who passed last year. I definitely wasn't thinking. I was reacting."

"Hey, there! Looks like some candles got out of control, or maybe you used too many lights on your tree," the bald-headed neighbor said as he approached the huddled family. "Sorry, that was rude. I was out walking the dog a few minutes ago when he ran toward your house and started barking like crazy. I guess he never forgot his old companion training. He used to be my dad's service dog. When Dad died, we sort of inherited him. Oh, and I had my phone with me, so I called the fire department right away."

Kaboom!

All five of the neighbors jumped back at the loud explosion from the house.

"Sounds like the gas tank on the car caught fire," the neighbor said.

"Not likely," Arlie replied. "That only happens in the movies, not real life. I'd say there was a bomb in there that got delayed. And no, we didn't have any candles and all the decorative lights were LEDs, so no heat. I'd say what we have here is a flaming case of arson."

***

"Thanks, Detective Biggar," the fire marshal said as he shook Arlie's hand. "We have lots of fires this time of year—mostly space heaters and overworked electrical outlets—but from what you just told me, your place was low risk. And you're sure the smoke detectors were working?"

"Yes, sir. We let the boys open their Christmas presents early. We were short one nine-volt battery. I looked up at the smoke alarm out of habit, saw the light blinking away at me, but told Carlos we'd have to wait to get a battery for that toy. I didn't check all the smoke alarms in the house, but I do know the one downstairs and the one in the master bedroom upstairs had lights blinking before I went to bed. I awoke to the smell of smoke, but no shrieking alarms. I guess it doesn't make a difference now. Everything is charcoal except the clothes on our backs." Arlie looked down at his bare belly, glad that he had grabbed the pair of Santa boxers on the way downstairs. "Or less," he added.

"The disaster relief folks are on their way now. They'll get you set up with a motel for the night and a few incidentals. You can contact your home owner's insurance company in the morning." The fire marshal looked at his watch and snorted. "Hmm. I guess you'll have to wait an extra day or two. It's Christmas in about fifteen minutes. They'll be closed."

"Well, I have my family, and that's what's most important."

"Oh, looks like the Red Cross crew are here now. Give me a call if you remember anything that would help in the investigation." He gave Arlie his card. "And as soon as you get a phone, let me know your number."

***

News item: Family flees flames on Christmas Eve. Just moments before midnight, a young couple and their two sons escaped a three-alarm fire in East Mesa. No one was injured. The house and all its contents were a total loss. The incident is under investigation.

"How'd they get that picture? I didn't see any cameras." Charlene said.

"Must have been one of the neighbors," Arlie said, then took the newspaper she handed him. "By the angle, I'd say it was someone in one of the two houses to the south of us. Everyone wants to be a news reporter nowadays. Thank goodness no names were used."

Charlene cocked her head to one side, confused.

"It's a newspaper! Names are supposed to be part of the news story, but I asked the fire marshal to keep that part hush-hush. I told him we're working on a sensitive case right now. I sorta dropped my name and association with the Anchorage Police Department, and mentioned the debacle last week at the park. When I raised my arm and flashed my leftover wounds from my cactus cartwheels, he remembered hearing about the confrontation and arrest of the De Lucas, and that was that."

"So, what are we going to do now?"

"Paw through these bags of donated clothes to see if there's anything to make ourselves decent, then go downstairs to the lobby and have a continental breakfast."

"Duh! I mean after we eat."

Arlie blew out a lungful of air, then reached into the top drawer on the hotel's dresser. "Ah, pen and paper. Let's make a list."

"Make two lists. I'm sure what's on your to-do list will be a lot different than mine. For me, would you write down call the property management company?"

"Yes, ma'am!" Arlie said brightly, then crossed one foot over his knee. "I knew my secretarial skills would come in handy one day."

"And for your list, dear husband-to-be, get some real pants. And quick! The boys will be awake soon and your Santa looks like a Pinocchio!"

"Oops!" Arlie rearranged his bits and pieces, then looked at her and smiled. "And just for the record, I'm a briefs kind of guy, not boxers, and you can see why."

"I certainly can," Charlene said, then giggled and looked at the queen-sized bed where the boys were asleep, curled together like two Irish Setter puppies in a cardboard box.

"What's so funny?"

Charlene got up and stood behind him. She hugged him around his shoulders and kissed him gently on his neck beneath his ear. She whispered, "I found a spot that the cactus missed," then kissed it again. "What I thought was so funny was how much life has changed since you came into our lives."

"Okay…" *Yeah, keep it neutral and see what she has to say. Don't jump in about her losing a home and a job!*

"Let's see. Well, I found out that my son's new best friend at school is really is half-brother, and I got to find out what a wonderful man their biological father is. I suddenly became financially able to quit my job..."

Arlie watched as she pulled away, emotionally and physically. The loss of her warmth felt as if he'd been stripped of half his gut. "What?"

And then he realized why she looked so stunned.

"Come back here and sit down." He patted his lap. "This is serious, so Pinocchio should stay put."

Charlene settled in his lap and rested the side of her head on the top of his, her eyes not on him, but on the sleeping boys.

"Yes, all that money Rosa left you to take care of him is gone. I don't know where you stashed it, but unless it was in a fireproof safe, it's ash. She may have had a renter's insurance policy on the house which would cover the contents, but not any large sums of cash. Even if she didn't have insurance, you still have me. I'm not a millionaire, but I'm not a pauper by any means. If you remember," he nuzzled her neck, "I already agreed to take care of you and the boys."

He kissed her shoulder gently, then pulled back. "Fess up time for me. I was actually kind of hurt that you didn't need me, that you were suddenly rich. I was afraid to ask you to marry me after you told me about the money she left for the care of Carlos, stashed in a big dog food bag."

"Really? You think I'd marry you for money?"

"No," Arlie said, trying not to be offended by her sharp tone, "I never thought that for a second. I was afraid, though, that you thought that I'd be marrying *you* for the money."

Charlene laughed, then kissed him soundly. "We'll be fine, one way or another. I think I'll wake up the boys, though. I'm hungry. Here, look through this bag. It's full of various sizes of sweats. I already found some for me. Too bad about losing all those fancy bras Rosa had."

"Yeah, I'll agree on that one," Arlie said. "Let's see what they have in here that'll fit me."

Charlene sat down on the bed next to Chip. "Mommy, are you still going to marry Arlie," he asked.

"Whoa, there! I didn't know you were already awake, you little possum. Yes, we're still going to get married. Why wouldn't we?"

"Because we don't have a house anymore. I know I didn't get to ride my new bike for very long, but Santa can get me another one. I just want to make sure I still have a daddy."

"Yeah, same here," Carlos said.

Knock, knock!

Arlie quickly added the matching gray sweatshirt to his new *ensemble* and answered the door.

"Here you go, sir. The Red Cross lady dropped these by. She said you'd probably want these right away."

The desk clerk handed Arlie a bundle of shoe boxes, tied together with twine. "She said these should work until you got a chance to do some shopping. And she also gave me this Sprawl-Mart gift card to help you get some of the essentials; at least until you got your financials straightened out."

The clerk shrugged his shoulder. "You're not the first family we've helped put up, so I'll tell you right now, the one thing most folks miss most is their phone. The little gas station mini market on the corner is open today. You can buy one of those little no-contract phones there. Oh, and to help you have a merry Christmas, we're having a fancier than normal brunch today."

"Are you one of Santa's elves?" Carlos asked. "I think I saw you at the mall last week."

The clerk chuckled. "Yeah, I help Santa when he comes to town. And I'll tell you a secret. If all your presents burned up in the fire, all you have to do is let one of the helpers he left behind know which one was your favorite and he'll see if Santa can replace it."

"So, are you one of those helpers?" Chip asked.

"Yes, I am. Just have your mom or dad help you write it down and I'll see what Santa has left."

The clerk looked up at Arlie and grinned. "My church helps out a lot, too. After you've had breakfast and get a phone, everything else should be a breeze. At least you have clothes on your back now."

Arlie nodded to the shoe boxes and said, "And shoes on our feet." He reached out and shook the young man's hand. "We appreciate all you've done." He turned to the boys. "Do your bathroom stuff—one at a time—and then it's breakfast!"

***

"So, where to now? I'd say go to my old place, but I sort of," Charlene brought the Styrofoam cup up to her lips and mumbled, "burned my bridges there."

Arlie copied her coy 'hide behind the coffee cup' tactic, then nodded, waiting for her to explain.

"The landlord was always trying to hit on me. I put up with it for a long time because I didn't want to lose my apartment. but then I realized I didn't have to anymore. While you were in the hospital, I told him I was giving him thirty days notice and he started in again. 'I'm going to miss your smiling face,' he said, and grabbed my hand and brought it up to kiss it.

"I won't go into details, but I told him off big time. I had Rosa's big house pre-paid for almost a year and her 'child support' endowment: all those dog food bagged-dollars for when the lease ran out. I probably lost my security and cleaning deposits by cussing him out, but I didn't care. Still don't."

Charlene huffed as she recalled the encounter. She shook her head as several other bad memories came to mind. "That ass! Why are men always trying to dominate me?"

"Am I?"

"No, you're different. I never got that vibe from you." Charlene took another sip of coffee, then set down the cup. "Sorry about snapping at you. Yes, you're different in a good way."

"Thanks. I think it's because to dominate, one person has to step on top of the other. I want to be by your side—be a team. If you yoke a team of oxen—have them work together, side by side—you'll get more work done than if you stack one on top of the other."

"True," Charlene said, then giggled. "But then again, it sounds like the other way could be fun."

"Yeah, well, we can work side by side during the day, then try one of top of the other for recreational purposes after the boys are asleep."

Chapter 4
Pirates

Pirate trivia: Every pirate ship had its own set of rules including how stolen loot (often food, lumber, cloth and animal hides, but seldom gold and gems) would be divided, who did which chores, and rules about how arguments would be settled.

"That didn't take long," Charlene said when Arlie walked through the door.

"The mini market is just around the corner and it wasn't busy."

"Daddy's back, Daddy's back," the boys chorused.

"Is everyone up for an adventure?" Arlie asked, both hands behind his back.

"I am! I am!" Chip exclaimed.

"Me, too," Carlos added, then whispered to Chip, "What's an adventure?"

"We're going to live in an itty-bitty house for a while. Your mother and I discussed it, and we're going to stay at my old home. Well, it isn't very old, but it is tiny… You might be able to visit Davey from school while we're there, too. His grandpa lives next door to me."

"Yay! Yay!"

"Well, that was easy enough," Charlene said.

"Yeah, well it shouldn't be too crowded since we don't have much of anything. I was thinking about getting the boys new bikes, but I don't want to acquire much in the way of worldly goods until we decide where we're going."

"Going?" Charlene asked, then turned to the boys. "Um, I think it's snack time. Why don't you two go see if they still have some fruit left in the dining area? I think an apple sounds good, don't you?"

"You just want us to leave so you can talk to Daddy by yourself," Chip said, with a pout.

"You can have an apple, but I want a 'nana," Carlos said, and grabbed his brother by the arm. "Come on. Let the big people talk... It's probably boring stuff, anyhow."

The boys skipped hand-in-hand into the wide common area the hotel used as a dining room. Charlene waited until they were out of earshot, then asked, "What's going on?"

"I didn't even have this new phone set up for one minute before Abby called me. She said the test results showed the syringe held xylazine, a horse sedative. The dosage was high enough that it would have killed me if all of it had been injected. I was lucky to get off with just sleeping for a day."

"And…"

"And given that it was probably a De Luca who administered it, I'd say it would be a good idea for us to get out of Dodge. Rather, Mesa. I'd like to go back to Alaska."

"Oh," Charlene said glumly. "I see," and looked away from him, dejected.

"Whoa! Whoa! Wait! I mean, I'd like *all* of us to go to Alaska. I'd be the only one going *back* to Alaska."

"Oh! Now I see." Charlene's eyes brightened, and a smile took over her pout. "But not really. You're wrong."

"Huh?"

"I'd be going *back*, too. I was at JBER, Fort Richardson, seven years ago. Actually, I kind of miss Alaska. The boys would probably love it. I don't think either of them have even seen snow up close, much less made a snowman. At least, it'll be novel for a while."

Arlie cleared his throat. "Fess up time. Again. I know I told you I was with the Anchorage Police Department, but I don't think I told you I left because I was on medical leave. Now that the bullet is out of my back and I'm not a cripple—

or at risk to be—I really should go back to work. I'll have more resources up there to find out what's going on, too. I really don't trust those crazy De Lucas not to come after Carlos again."

"Or you," Charlene said, and came in close, wrapped her arms around his neck, and kissed him gently. She pulled back and looked deep into his eyes, then scanned him head to toe with a grin. "Maybe tonight when the boys are asleep, I can give you an up close and personal examination. There might be a few more cactus thorns left that the jacuzzi and washcloth missed. I wouldn't want you to be uncomfortable on the flight back."

Arlie stepped closer and bent to nuzzle her neck. "So, are we staying here another night, or going to my itty-bitty trailer where the boys will be sleeping about two feet away?"

"I think you just answered your own question. Besides, this place has a full tub. I doubt yours has more than a stand-up shower, right?"

"True. And, by the time the boys get back with their snacks, I'll have figured out transportation to my place. My lemon-yellow Bug may look small on the outside, but it's plenty big for my family of four." Arlie's face scrunched up, deep in thought, then relaxed into a smile. "Big enough for my family *and* all our worldly possessions, too!"

***

"I really don't want to bring it up, and it's probably nothing, but just in case it's something you do all the time, I think we need to talk about it."

"What are you talking about?"

"About making life changing decisions that affect all of us by yourself without asking me first," Charlene said, then looked away, afraid to see how he'd taken her blunt reprimand.

"I'm sorry. I didn't mean to do that." He returned to watching the parking lot for the taxi he had called, then turned back to Charlene. "I really am sorry if I did that, but I swear, I don't remember where or when I did it. Would you fill me in?"

"Just a few minutes ago, when you told the boys we were moving to your itty-bitty trailer."

"Really? I mean, we had already decided that tonight would be our last night here, and you told me you slammed the door shut on the option for your old apartment, and we both know Rosa's rental burned to the ground literally at our feet. I figured the only option left open to us was staying at my place. I didn't think it was a topic for discussion, but then again, I've been pretty much single my entire adult life and may have missed the lesson on what needs to be discussed when in a relationship."

"Well, even if it's obvious, I'd feel a lot better if you and I talked about major decisions before telling the boys what we're going to do. As a parent, it's always been just me—no partner or co-parent—but I've read plenty of parenting books. One of the things you're never supposed to do is argue in front of the children."

"I'll agree with that one! I've seen enough of that in the line of duty."

Toot toot!

"That's my ride. Would you get the boys ready and gather all our worldly possessions? It shouldn't take me more than fifteen minutes, twenty minutes tops, to get my car and come back here."

The hairs on the back of Arlie's neck raised in fear that he had blown his chance with her, but he went ahead and kissed Charlene's cheek. "We'll get this figured out soon, I'm sure. While we're adjusting to our new lives, just remember,

71

I'll never do anything mean or vicious to you or the boys. Ever."

"All right. We'll be ready when you get back."

***

"We gotta tell them about the pirate's treasure," Chip whispered to Carlos.

"But we might get spanked," Carlos argued.

"Why would we get spanked?" Chip asked a little too loudly.

"All right, you two." Arlie said, as soon as he was in the door. He squatted down next to the boys. "What's going on?"

"We did something and we're afraid to tell you about it because you'll get mad at us. Carlos said he thought you'd spank us…" Chip said, then sniffed, trying not to cry.

"Did either of you pee in my coffee?" Arlie asked.

Both boys shook their heads.

"Did you stab someone with a stick?"

His sons shook their heads in tandem.

"Or hurt a dog or cat or other animal, just for fun?"

"Nuh uh!" They answered, then both crossed their arms in front of their chests, asserting their integrity while at the same time, hiding their secret even deeper.

"My turn," Charlene said. "Did either of you lie?"

"No," Chip said, then hung his head, "But we didn't tell you something."

Carlos nodded, agreeing with his brother, but remained mum.

"You mean you didn't tell me a secret?" Charlene asked.

"Uh huh. But if we tell you, will you get mad?" Carlos asked. "My other mother used to get real mad sometimes and yell and scream and it'd scare me. But then my nanny would come and get me, and I'd feel better, but Nana Maria's not here."

"Have you ever heard me yell or scream in anger, Carlos? And screaming at you to hide from bad guys doesn't count."

"My mom doesn't yell much," Chip said, his chest puffed out in pride.

"I'm his mom now, too, Chip, so that would be 'our mom doesn't yell much.' And Carlos, I don't spank little boys. The only time you'll get in trouble is for lying or being mean. Do you understand?"

"Uh huh," he replied, and dropped his hands to his side, ready to release his fear and his secret. "Okay, since you won't get mad 'cause we didn't lie or do anything mean, I'll tell you. You know all that money my mother—my first mother—left us in that big bag with the picture of a dog on the front?"

"Yes…" Arlie said, now crouched down beside Charlene, at eye level with the boys. *Don't feed him words! Let him tell you in his own way and time!*

Carlos kept his focus on Charlene, her hand gentle on his shoulder. "Well, I sorta forgot about it until Daddy told you he wanted to go back to Alaska. Then I remembered about the brown sack with Alaska written on it."

"Where was the sack?" Arlie prompted.

"When Chip and I opened up the dog food bag and packed the money into our treasure chests—those were the empty shoe boxes we found in the garage—we also found a bag with a bunch of papers and a picture in it. I told Chip it said Alaska, but he thought it said apples 'cause it started with an 'A.' But I can read pretty good, so I knew it said Alaska."

"Where is the Alaska sack now, Carlos?" Arlie asked, then stood up out of his crouch and stretched his back. "Let's go sit on the couch and talk about this where we'll be more comfortable."

"It's important, huh?" Chip asked and crawled up next to his new father.

"Yes, very important, so don't worry about telling me something you think might make me mad. I promise you, I won't get mad at you and I won't yell, either. I don't like to yell. It hurts my throat," Arlie added, then stuck out his tongue and grabbed his throat in mock pain, doing his best to bring up the mood of the interrogation of the two five-year-olds.

"Chip and I wanted to play pirates. We found the empty plastic boxes, but we didn't have a treasure to put in them. We got ready, though, and dug a hole in the backyard. But we still didn't have any gold or jewels. Then I remembered the money Mama left to take care of me, so we got it. Chip helped me fill our treasure chests with the money. I told him we had to take the Alaska bag, too, because it was a treasure map—we just didn't know how to read the clues yet."

"So, did you put *all* the money in the treasure chests or just some of it?" Charlene asked, then held her breath in anticipation.

Carlos hung his head down. "We put all the money in. It

was safer, too, 'cause only Chip and I knew where it was. We were gonna tell you and Daddy about it later, after Christmas. I just didn't want Alonzo De Luca..." *Pbbt!* Carlos pretended to spit, "to find it. It was hard to dig the holes at first, but Chip said he had a better idea. He said it would be easier if we dug up the flowers and put the money under them."

"Yeah, and then maybe the flowers would grow into money trees and we'd be billionaires!" Chip said with a big grin, very proud of his part in the gardening pirates adventure.

Charlene's smile and sigh enhanced her glow of relief. "We have money," she whispered to Arlie, then reached across and gave him a hug and a kiss on the cheek.

"And we may have evidence, too!" Arlie whispered back.

"So, does this mean we're going back to the old house to look around?" she asked.

"Yes, but let's do it tomorrow after we check out. That'll give the fire marshal and his crew a chance to finish their search for evidence. Besides, I need to buy a few things before we go there and most of the stores are closed today. So everyone, until it's time to go shopping, let's take the day off and just chill. Santa's elf said he had some cards and board games we could borrow. Our lives may get hectic pretty soon, so how about if we take today to get to know each other a little better?"

"What's heck it?" Carlos asked.

"Hectic means real busy, sometimes so busy you forget to think or be polite."

Chip and Carlos both nodded. "I know what that is," Chip said, "but Mommy just calls it being frazzled."

"Yes," Arlie said, and brought his hand up Charlene's back, then rubbed her gently between her shoulder blades. "Frazzled is a great word for hectic. Come on, let's go check out a few games."

***

The next morning

"We're ready," Charlene said when Arlie had finished showering. "Let's eat, then brave the post-Christmas shopping madness."

"Okay, Mom and boys. Let's go buy some fabric grocery bags and a shovel, and then go play pirate."

"She's not your Mom," Chip said.

"True, but she does answer to Mom, right?"

Carlos leaned over to Chip and whispered loud enough

for all to hear, "We can share her with him, too. She'll probably call him Dad sometimes, and that's okay, too."

"Go ahead down to the lobby and grab what you want for breakfast," Charlene said. "I want to talk to *Dad* for a moment."

Carlos and Chip rolled their eyes at the same time. Chip said, "Probably big people boring stuff, huh, Carlos?"

"Yeah, huh," he replied.

"I understand the shovel, but what are the bags for?" Charlene asked when they were out of earshot.

"Chances are the plastic shoe boxes the boys used were see-through. With all the snoopy and camera-happy neighbors in the neighborhood, I'm sure they'll be curious about why we're digging in the back yard. I think I'll grab some small trash bags, too."

"You're still not making any sense."

"I'll grab some used plastic bags out of the recycle box at the store and use them to wrap up the flowers you planted. We'll put the boxes of money in the colorful cloth bags, then plop a plastic-bagged flower on top. No one will know that we have boxes of money under the bagged petunias when we take them back to the car."

"They're pansies…"

"Still flowers…"

***

"We're here. It sure looks different than the last time we saw it," Arlie said, then looked at the boys in the back seat. "Wait here with your mother while I make sure it's safe to go around to the backyard."

"I wonder if my bike burned up?" Chip asked.

"Probably. Mine, too," Carlos added.

"Don't worry about either one of them. Bikes are replaceable. Besides, if we're going to Alaska, you can't ride bikes in the winter," Charlene said.

"Why not?" they both asked.

"Because where we're going, there's lots and lots of snow. You can't ride a bicycle in it, but we'll buy you sleds and maybe even ice skates."

"What are ice steaks?" Chip asked.

"Skates, not steaks. They're sort of like skateboards, but without the wheels. You put one on each foot like a shoe, and then you can glide over ice." Charlene illustrated skimming across the dashboard, her fingers moving back and forward like an ice skater.

"But where are we going to buy that much ice?" Carlos asked.

Charlene chuckled. "Don't worry about finding enough ice in Alaska in the winter. Believe me, there's no shortage." She looked up. "Dad's here. Let's hear what he has to say."

"Put on your digging gloves, mateys," he said in a pirate voice, then rolled an 'Arrgh!' at the end. "Captain Biggar will lead the way. Lassie," he said to Charlene, "Do ye want to join us or stay on the ship and be a look out?"

Charlene's mouth twisted out of a frown and into a smile. "Aye, I'll stay here and mind the mizzen masts and sheets. Ye and the lads take care and keep yer powder dry…" She switched back to plain English. "I'll call your phone if someone's coming. Don't answer: just run or hide, whichever is easier."

"Are you okay," Arlie whispered while the boys tried to put their fingers in the right places in the gardening gloves.

"Yeah, it's just you looked like my dad when you did that pirate impersonation."

"Your dad? I'd like to meet him someday. I've never met anyone—other than the boys—who looked like me."

Charlene shook her head emphatically, her lips pursed

in absolute denial.

"O-kay…"

"What's that supposed to mean," she snapped in a hoarse whisper.

"As a professional interrogator, I'd say that means your father is still alive, but you're not on the best of terms and really don't want to talk to or about him."

Charlene shrugged her shoulder and sniffed. 'Where's a box of tissues when you need one?' she asked, then bent forward to search the floorboards of the front and back seats, intentionally hiding her face and her freshly sprouted tears.

You know she doesn't want an answer. She'd probably lash out at you if you did know where any were, so keep your mouth shut and attitude upbeat for the boys.

"Come on, mateys," Arlie said to his sons. "Our quartermaster has her own duty as lookout and seeker of the disposable handkerchiefs."

Just as Chip was set to ask what those were, Carlos brought up his gloved hand and pretended to blow his nose. "Oh," Chip said, "Mom needs a Kleenex."

***

Arlie walked over the trampled barricade tape into the

gated backyard. The stucco fence was intact, but now streaked black and steel gray instead of solid creamy white. "Stay in my footprints, boys. There's broken glass in places." He walked through the charcoal and ash remains of the once opulent patio to the untouched flower garden that Rosa had started and Charlene had 'flowered.'

Arlie was impressed. The boys had done a great job of covering their booty. He could tell where the decorative bark had been disturbed, but chances were, the arsonist didn't have a reason to inspect the backyard landscape for hidden treasures before setting up his fiery trap and disabling the door locks from the outside.

"Where's the first one?"

"We started right here," Carlos said. "I made sure it looked just like before. Mama used to do this all the time. She told me I always had to cover my tracks, even though I didn't have a car."

The poor kid! He's probably been living under surveillance and suspicion his whole life! Rosa probably taught him more than any five-year-old needed to know about survival in a mobster's world.

"I'll dig and you two pack the flowers up nice and pretty."

Arlie made quick work digging the plastic boxes out of the loose soil. The boys brushed the dirt off each one, stacked them in the cloth shopping bags, then topped each sack with clumps of bagged pansies.

"Almost done?" Charlene asked, startling Arlie and the boys who had been intent on their packaging.

Arlie nodded, then out of habit, shifted his stance to look behind her.

"It's just me. The street's deserted."

Picking up the dirt-smudged envelope, Arlie said, "Sorry mates, but I need to study this treasure map first. I'll figure out the clues, then let you know if it leads to gold or jewels or if it's just a bill for shipping salmon to Alaska."

"Shipping salmon to Alaska?" Charlene asked with a chuckle, her upbeat tone indicating she was ready to come back to the real world, willing to desert the pain of recalling problems she had, or once had, with her father.

Arlie opened the envelope and quickly leafed through the documents, then stopped when he came to the photo. "Crap. I know this man. I'm going to have to check this out. How about we finish up here pronto? Knock off as much dirt as you can from the outside of the bags, too. I don't want to be hosing these off at the trailer. Lots of eyes around there, too."

"Who is it?" Charlene asked.

"No one you'd know, I'm sure," he replied. "But by the looks of some of these notes, he's in danger. Come on, boys, gloves off, smack 'em together to clean 'em up a bit, then let's go to our next new home!"

Charlene laughed out loud. "This will be, what, the fourth place you've slept in the last week?"

"Let's see: hospital, here, hotel, then back to the itty-bitty home again. I guess you're right. Oh, and when we get back to the trailer, would you get online and see if you can find four one-way tickets to Alaska while I look over these?"

Arlie's face reddened as he realized what he had just done. "I mean, if you and the boys want to come up to Alaska with me. It's cold and we'll have to get a whole new wardrobe..."

Charlene tucked her chin to her chest and pierced him with her 'are you kidding me?' stare.

"Oh, yeah. We'll have to get a new wardrobe whether we go to Alaska or Hawaii or stay here in Mesa." Arlie put the documents and photo back in the envelope. "So, does this mean you want to come with me?"

"I can't imagine staying here without you. How'd this happen so quickly?"

"I don't know. I'm just glad it did." Arlie wiped a spot of dirt off Charlene's cheek with his fingertip, then kissed her on the cleaned spot.

"You missed," she said, then grabbed him by the back of the neck and kissed him like she hadn't seen him in a year. "Sorry I was so short with you earlier. Not being able to make my own decisions—or voice my own opinions—is a flash anger point for me. I know you'd never try to dominate me, and we're working with some high intensity issues here, so my emotions are about," Charlene held the tips of her thumb and forefinger together about a hair-width apart, "this far beneath my skin."

"Well," Arlie said, and brought her visual example up to his mouth, "As long as we keep talking, we'll be fine. There's nothing we can't work out together, but I flunked out of my ESP class. You'll have to talk to me because I can't read your mind. Same goes for you, too. If I'm playing it too close to the chest—or you feel as if I'm shutting you out—please tell me. I'm not doing it on purpose."

Charlene sneaked a hand up his shirt without the boys seeing what she was doing, rubbed his sparse chest hairs, then tickled his nipple, causing him to flinch. "I promise I'll let you know. And I'll do it without a pissy attitude."

Arlie kissed her on the tip of her nose. "Back at ya, darling."

***

"Now what are we going to do with all this money?" Charlene asked, stacking the last of the plastic containers under the kitchen sink.

Arlie looked at her, shook his head, and chuckled.

"Pbbt! That's something I never thought I'd hear myself say!" she replied.

"I'm glad the banks are open today. We can deposit some of it, but for the rest of it, that's why I picked up all these postal flat rate boxes."

"Explain, please, my dear."

"You can only put so much money into a bank account before they start asking for social security numbers and such. I'd tell you to put it all in the bank, but then the government would want to know where it all came from. Put some of it in your bank, then open one or two new accounts at other banks—and open a few accounts for Chip at the same time, listing yourself as guardian. Put $9,000 into each of the accounts. Pack up the rest in the flat rate boxes. We can mail them to my PO box in Anchorage. I'll put some of the cash in my two accounts and stash the rest in a safety deposit box, but Carlos is out when it comes to this."

"Why can't I open a bank account for him?"

"No documentation. You don't have a birth certificate for him, and I won't chance using Chip's. Plus, I doubt he has a social security number. He was born in Costa Rica to a mother who was a felon married to a mobster P.O.S. Our young Carlos is a non-entity right now, totally off anyone's radar, except the De Lucas. He doesn't exist as far as the U.S. government is concerned. Rosa was a clever cyber-criminal. She figured out identity theft before she was even out of high school. I'm sure she dummied up a passport for him to get to the states. That piece of ID is gone with the ashy wind, I'm sure."

"Can you fix that, I mean, make him legitimate?" Charlene asked.

"I'll do something later, but right now there are too many other rumbling issues that need to be taken care of, like getting airplane tickets, moving money around, and saving a life." Arlie held up the Alaska envelope that held evidence and the name and photo of a man on the De Luca's hit list. "Let me make a few calls while you find tickets. And if you can, route us through Portland instead of Seattle. That airport is a blast for travelers of any age."

Chapter 5

Ted Stevens Anchorage International Airport, located just a few miles from downtown Anchorage, Alaska, is one of the world's busiest international cargo airports, generally in the top five rated in the world. Portland International Airport is often ranked number one in overall customer satisfaction when rated by JD Power and remains a popular airport, scoring high for their customer services and amenities, according to other surveys.

Carlos tugged on Arlie's sleeve. "Can I get a haircut?" he asked meekly. "There's a barber shop right here and you said our plane doesn't leave for another three hours."

"Ahh," Charlene crooned, as she tickled her blushing fiancé in the ribs. "You get to witness your son's first haircut."

"Not exactly his first haircut, but yes, it will be the first one I've ever seen." He took Carlos's hand and said, "Sure, son. Let's go in and see if there's a wait."

"Good afternoon folks," the rainbow-hued hair stylist said. "Who gets the honor, or are all of you here for a new look?"

"Just the one son. Tell her what you want, Carlos," Arlie

said, adding a wink to the shy boy.

Carlos asked him, "Can I get it however I want?" then shook his head, erasing his former life of looking like and wearing whatever someone else dictated.

"Whatever you want. Just remember, it's going to take a while to grow out, so I'd advise against a Mohawk."

"I want it to look just like his," Carlos told the stylist and pointed to Chip.

The young stylist with eyeshadow the same color purple as her bangs looked from one boy to the other. "Well, that might be tough. How about if I give both of you a fresh haircut? Then they'll be identical."

"Chip, do you want a haircut, too?" Charlene asked.

"You bet! Then everyone will know we're brothers, even if we aren't twins."

"Step up here and sit on this booster. I'll get you first, then your brother." The stylist looked at Arlie then Charlene, not even trying to hide her curiosity about how the boys could look so much alike, then realized that by asking, she might be missing a tip.

"It's complicated," Charlene whispered, staving off the unspoken question, then returned to her normal voice. "Just don't get it too short. We're on our way to Alaska."

"They have adorable knit caps at practically every shop here. Even without fresh haircuts, they'd need them." The stylist switched on the clippers. "Now hold still. I promise this won't hurt, and I'll be done in a jif."

"Thanks," Arlie said when both boys were done. He handed the bubbly barber a couple of bills to cover the haircuts and a bit extra to pay for the shopping advice. "Now, boys, let's go get some hats!"

***

Ding! Ding!

"Now arriving at Ted Stephens Anchorage International Airport where the local time is eleven PM. The current temperature outside is twelve degrees above zero. Please keep your seat belts…"

"Now that was an easy flight," Arlie said to Charlene, seated across the aisle from him.

"I can't believe they slept the whole way through. I hope that won't mess them up for sleeping tonight."

"Are we in Alaska yet?" Chip asked, suddenly sitting up straight, wide awake with excitement.

"Yes, we are. It'll take a while for us to get off the plane, then we'll have to wait for that box of hats and hoodies we bought to get up to baggage claim, but we're here."

Carlos, now awake, too, pressed his face to the window and looked out. "There're lots of lights out there, but it's still so dark! And everybody's wearing so many clothes! Look at those guys! They have hats and gloves and big coats... Hey, are they smoking? I thought smoking was illegal."

Arlie looked out over Carlos's shoulder. "Yes, they have lots and lots of clothes on because it's so cold. Smoking isn't illegal everywhere, but they're not smoking. What you're seeing is their breath."

"Huh?" Carlos asked.

"Yeah, huh?" Chip echoed.

"Just wait. Your dad and I will show you all about it when we get out of the airport."

***

"Well, this is convenient," Arlie said, as he herded his family into the airport terminal tourist shop. "These heavy-weight Alaska-emblazoned jackets should work for all of you. Your new sneakers will get you to my car, but you'll need to get snow boots eventually."

"What about you?" Charlene asked, pulling the thin

92

polyester fabric of his jacket away from his arm.

"This will work for right now. I have a storage unit with my winter gear and just about everything else I own in it...which isn't much. I guess you'll have to..."

Ask, don't assume, idiot!

Arlie faked a cough and started his sentence again. "I guess we'll have to figure out something, so you and the boys can get new winter wardrobes."

Charlene chuckled. "Good save there, Dad. Yes, I'm sure we'll get the clothes and shoe shopping chores sorted out. I think you have enough on your plate already, though. How about if the lady ox takes the boys out tomorrow?"

"Moo, moo! That means yes in ox-talk," Arlie said, then kissed her cheek. "We're a great team. No yoke required."

Chip reached up and grabbed onto her hand. "I'm still hungry, Mommy."

"Me, too," Carlos agreed, and came around to take her other hand.

"Why don't you and the boys get something to eat?" Arlie asked. "I'll go wait downstairs for our box."

"I smell cinnamon rolls!" Chip shouted.

"Maybe they have ice cream, too," Carlos added. "Now

I'm real hungry!"

Arlie gave Charlene a quick kiss on the lips. "Just go down the escalator and follow the signs to baggage claim. I'll wait for you there," then he took off.

As he rode the escalator down, scanning the multitudes of faces traveling in the middle of the night, Arlie recognized the man from the hit contract photo. He quickly walked up the down escalator to intercept the man before he and his companion got to security.

Evidently, the older gentleman and the younger woman at his side had decided to get some exercise before their flight and were using the stairs instead of the escalator. "Excuse me, Judge Taylor," Arlie called out as he rushed up behind the couple, stopping them just before they entered the pre-check security line. "I have to talk with you, sir. It's very important."

The man and woman stopped and turned around. "Detective Biggar?" the man asked, certain of who he was speaking to, but curious about why he was chasing him down at the airport.

"Yes, sir. Good evening, ma'am," Arlie said, nodding to the woman holding onto the silver-haired gentleman's elbow.

94

"If I could just have a couple moments of your time, your honor."

"Well, Arlie, I can tell by the frantic look on your face that this is important." He turned to his wife. "Come on, dear. Let's go over here where we're not so conspicuous," and led the trio to the alcove under the escalators.

As soon as the foot traffic passed and the three were alone, Arlie started in. "I don't know if you know, sir, but I had to take a medical leave from the police department, courtesy of the De Luca brothers. While I was recuperating in Arizona, I ran into them again. After an extremely aggravated encounter between them and my family, the De Luca brothers were locked up for attempted murder, courtesy of the Pinal County Sheriff. There's more to the story, and it gets complicated, but the short version is, I found evidence that they put a contract out on you. The De Lucas want you dead."

"Oh, my," escaped the woman's lips just as her hand flew up to cover her mouth. "Sorry. I know this isn't the first time there have been rumors of a contract out for you, but it's the first time I've heard about it at the same time you did."

The judge patted her hand. "Don't worry about it. Right

now, only a few people know I'm leaving the state, and even fewer know my final destination."

Arlie waited while the judge reassured his wife, then spoke up. "I found your picture in an envelope along with some other papers. I think they're the missing documents we've been looking for."

"Get them to the district attorney and they'll go from there. In the meantime, my new wife and I are on our way to Hawaii. My vacation time has been scheduled for months, but leaving the state was spontaneous, just like everything else in our lives seems to be."

"How many people know you're leaving?" Arlie asked.

"I had my secretary make sure my docket was cleared until the end of January and any questions for me were to be held until I returned or referred to another judge. I didn't say whether I was traveling Outside or having a staycation at home. Either way, it was and is my intention to treat myself to two weeks without *any* harassment," Judge Taylor said, then added a nod of finality.

"Other than mine," his young wife said, poking him in the ribs.

"Yes," he said and sighed with a good-humored grin of

surrender on his face. "She insists I try a few traditional Hawaiian foods and activities while we're there. Can you imagine a fifty-two-year old man, riding the waves with nothing but a length of polished wood under his feet?"

"Yes, actually I can," Arlie said with a chuckle. "I have a question, though. Do they waterproof the training wheels they put on your surfboard?"

The three shared a big laugh, then Arlie heard the boys bickering about who had more gummy worms on his yogurt.

"Oh, here they are, my sons and fiancée. Too bad you're leaving town. You could have performed the ceremony."

"Grandpa!" Chip shouted as he ran up to give Judge Taylor a one-armed tackle hug, his candied yogurt held out for Arlie to take so he could make it a full wrap-around snuggle.

Carlos looked up at Charlene as they slowly approached the reunited family. "Is he my grandpa, Mommy?"

"Yes, he is," she said, then took a deep bracing breath. "Come on, let me introduce you."

Carlos clutched Charlene's hand as she chewed her bottom lip in anticipation of the inescapable reunion with the father she had shunned two years earlier.

"Hi, Dad. Hi, Lara."

The judge's head looked back from his daughter to Arlie and then down to the young boy who could be a twin to the one he was holding in his arms. "Charlene? I don't understand…"

"Dad, before I even begin to explain, I want to say I'm sorry to both of you for being such a snob. I should have accepted Lara right off the bat. I understand love at first sight now. I thought it was just a myth, something to be used for songs and stories to exploit the masses. Now, as you see, I've fallen in love at first sight with these two adorable men. It looks as if you already know Arlie, but this is our other son, Carlos."

Carlos reached out his hand. "Glad to meet you, sir."

The judge squatted down and opened out his other arm. "I'm your grandpa, Carlos. You can call me Grandpa or Pappy or Gramps or whatever you like." The judge looked up at Arlie, then lifted Carlos as he stood up, now holding both of his grandsons. "And here I thought Chip got his red hair and brown eyes from me. We can catch up later, but I'm not assuming too much when I say that you're the boys' biological father, right?"

Arlie nodded as Charlene came in close and snuggled under his arm to take a hug from her very willing fiancé. "The evidence is before you, your honor."

***

"That's ours, that's ours!" Chip cried out, pointing to the brightly colored box on the luggage carousel.

"Now we can finally leave the airport. I'm sorry to say it, but we'll be in a hotel again for a few more nights."

"Don't you have an itty-bitty trailer here, too, Daddy?" Carlos asked.

"Nope. I had even less of a home than that before I came to Arizona. I had a roommate and we shared a two-bedroom apartment. He has someone else living with him now. Don't worry, though. Your mom and I will find us a great place, I'm sure. I have a friend who said he has a house in Chugiak he'll rent us if we all like it."

"Is that where Chewbacca lives?" Carlos asked.

"Chewbacca? Why, what..."

"Chugiak, Chewbacca..." Charlene prompted Arlie, then laughed. "No, Chewbacca doesn't live in Chugiak, but he'd fit right in. Lots of other furry critters live there—most of them are sled dogs, though. I don't think there are any alien space pilots, but I'm not sure"

Chirp! Chirp!

"What was that?" Charlene asked Arlie.

"That's the remote start on my car. See that red monster over there, the one with smoke coming out the tailpipe?"

"You own a Hummer?"

"I bought it when I thought I'd be able to go fishing and hunting. Turned out that all the fishing I did was for clues and hunting was for bad guys. This isn't exactly low profile, but it does great getting around in weather like this. I had thought about selling it before I left, but decided to wait and see if I came back or not. Turns out, it could be the perfect family car."

"Wow! You mean that's our car?" Chip asked, his faced pressed against the plate glass window, looking out into the parking garage.

"Yes, it is, but don't go outside yet. I'll drive up to the door, and then you can get in. Now, a couple of quick lessons about winter here. First, when it's cold out like this, remember to always breathe through your nose. Keep your mouth closed or it'll freeze your throat, or at least feel like it."

Chip and Carlos brought their hands up to their mouths

at the same time, covering them with their new gloves. "And what else?" Carlos mumbled through his polar-fleeced fingers.

"Don't touch metal outside with bare hands. And definitely don't lick it! The moisture will freeze almost immediately, freezing your hand—or tongue—to whatever you're touching. Oh, and never run on ice! It's slick and you'll probably fall. Beware of shiny ground. It's sure to be slippery!"

"Huh?"

"Arlie, I'll help them out. Don't scare them before they've even left the building. But boys, this is going to be like living on another planet."

"Like where Chewbacca was where they had all the snow monsters?"

"Something like that," Charlene said, then looked over at Arlie as he swiped the screen on his phone. "What are you doing now? The car's already running."

"Checking for bugs. I'll be right back."

Arlie left the terminal and approached his car, holding his phone like it was a phaser and he was scanning for alien life forms. "Aha!" He zeroed in on an area just above the tailpipe, then ran his hand above the inside of the truck body. "Gotcha!"

He looked over the button-sized device, then rubbed his thumb across the top of it to clear away the road grime. He set it on a nearby trash can and snapped pictures of it on all sides. "How about a bit of burger," he said to it softly, as if the device was a person. He pulled a fast food wrapper from the garbage can, folded it around the tracking device, then returned the trash-wrapped parcel to the garbage. "This ought to have the bad guys making a trip to the landfill in a day or two."

Arlie sighed as he climbed into the pre-warmed driver's seat. "No more back pain," then pulled in front of the parking garage entrance to the terminal.

"Look at me, boys," he said as he put his fingers over his mouth like he was going to throw a kiss. He pulled away his hand and exhaled. "See? No, it's not smoke. It's the warm moisture from my breath turning into instant fog. Or something like that. Remember, breathe through your nose!"

He opened the doors for Charlene and the boys, then loaded the box of cold weather gear into the back of his rig. "Let's go. It's tomorrow already and I haven't been to sleep yet."

Charlene asked the boys, "Did you buckle up?" then turned to Arlie and whispered hoarsely, "Why were you talking to my dad?"

"Wow! You don't beat around the bush, do you?" Arlie turned back to the boys. "Did you figure out those seatbelts or do you need a hand?"

"We got it!" Chip said, then snuggled close to Carlos. "This is fun! I've never been really cold before."

"Me neither," Carlos said. "It never got cold in Costa Rica."

Arlie turned back to Charlene. "Can this wait for a little bit? They'll probably be asleep before we get to the motel."

"Nope. I mean, nope, I don't beat around the bush, but yes, I guess I can wait a few minutes. I'm not surprised you know Dad since he's a judge and you're a detective in his district, but why now? It didn't look like it was a casual conversation, either. Lara looked scared."

Arlie stifled his groan of defeat—she wasn't going to back off—and turned it into clearing his throat. "First off, I had no idea he was your father. You do realize, I believe, that you have different last names. I was going to explain later, but wow! What a surprise! Judge Taylor is your father."

"I took my mother's name when he was just starting out as a lawyer, just in case some idiot had a grudge and wanted to take it out on me or my mother, God rest her soul."

"So, Lara isn't your mother?"

Charlene shook her head and pursed her lips, biting off any smart aleck remarks about did she look anything like that curvy blonde who was only five years older than her?

Arlie ignored the 'look' and continued to the parking lot exit. "Anyhow, I didn't want the boys to see you upset." He put the car in park while he waited for the vehicles ahead of him to get through the exit, took a deep breath, and looked deep into her eyes, making sure she was listening to him and not fuming over her father's decision to remarry a younger woman. "Your dad is the hit. It was his photo in the envelope the boys found with Alaska written on it. I'm just glad Chip didn't look inside and see it."

Charlene groaned as she realized she was on the offensive again, and hadn't given Arlie credit for using discretion in a sensitive situation. "Sorry," she said softly and placed her hand on his elbow.

"Shit!" she exclaimed, then looked back to see if the

boys were awake and had heard.

They were both zonked out, leaning on each other like Siamese twins joined at the pompoms of their knit caps. She turned back as Arlie put the car back in drive and waved his badge to get through.

He looked in the rearview mirror and verified the boys were asleep. "Yeah, shit," he agreed. "And I found a bug on this vehicle when I was in the parking garage. Looks like we're getting a new ride. Even without the tracker, a Chinese Cherry Red Hummer isn't hard to spot. Feel like getting a new minivan, Mom?"

"Yeah, well, around here a minivan would be like hiding a zebra in a herd of zebras. Or a white car in Arizona. Good idea, but one of the first things I want to do is renew my concealed weapons permit...and find out if we could get bullet-proof windows and solid tires for our new ride. I grew up a bit wary because of Dad's position, but I wasn't protecting a family, my family."

Arlie patted her leg. "That certainly puts a whole new spin on 'to protect and to serve' for me, too."

Chapter 6

Knock! Knock!

"Well, good morning, Marc. How'd you know I was back?"

"Who is it, dear, and would you either invite him in or step outside? You're letting in all the cold air!" Charlene grabbed her hoodie from the back of the chair and threw it on over her long-sleeved shirt.

"I think it feels good!" Chip crowed. "It's like you have the air conditioning on full blast and don't have to worry about the electric bill, huh, Mom?"

"Come on inside, Marc, and meet my family. This is Charlene Barbour, my fiancée, and our two sons, Chip and Carlos."

Marc's eyes widened as he looked from the boys to Arlie, and then back again twice. He shrugged his shoulder but didn't say a word. He'd known Arlie since college and his sometimes partner in undercover operations had never mentioned having children, much less a fiancée.

"Yeah," Arlie said, "I know, they look just like me."

"It's complicated," Charlene whispered to the stunned man, then spoke up. "Glad to meet you, Marc."

"You look familiar…"

"You do, too. Were you ever attached to JBER?"

Marc chuckled and answered, "That's classified, on a need to know basis," then winked.

"Oh, I see… I was with JAG a few years ago." She looked at Chip, did the quick math for his age, pregnancy, and when she was artificially inseminated, and amended, "Almost seven years ago."

"Maybe I saw you around back then. So, how did you wind up with this rascal?" Marc asked, then did a double-take when he saw Arlie wrestling on the bed with Chip and Carlos.

"Fate," she replied. "I was in Arizona and we kept bumping into each other."

Marc tried to swallow his sly smile, but Charlene had seen it. Marc knew Arlie was clever with his undercover talents and 'accidental' encounters were usually planned.

"You're looking good, Arlie. How'd you get rid of that bullet?" he asked, making sure he changed the subject in case she had been under surveillance and didn't know it.

"Santa gave me a magic utility belt for an early

Christmas present," Arlie said, then tickled Carlos and stood up to avoid getting the same in return.

"Huh?"

"My trailer park neighbor constructed a Velcro belt with ultra-high-powered magnets in it. One of the magnets pulled that slug away from my spine—stopping short of yanking it right through the skin—then it did double duty as a bullet-proof cummerbund when I was shot in the back, again, by Alonzo De Luca."

Charlene stood up and joined the conversation. "I keep forgetting to ask you about that. I thought bullet slugs were made of lead."

"The one he used was steel-encased, thank You, Lord," Arlie said. "I'm kinda, sorta glad I got shot, though."

"Okay, time for a brain scan," Marc said, and playfully tugged on Arlie's elbow, trying to lead him to the door.

"No, no, wait. If I hadn't been shot, I wouldn't have been half-crippled and gone to Arizona to avoid the icy Alaskan parking lots and sidewalks. And if I hadn't been bored out of my gourd and gone job hunting…"

Charlene cleared her throat and both men looked at her.

"The first time we met was at the Christmas carnival. I

guess we can thank Dave, the magic utility belt manufacturer, for getting you to volunteer," she said.

"Actually, the first time we met was at Sprawl-Mart, just after my job interview. You were working in the crafts department. You gave me instructions on how to make slipcovers for pillows, then sold me the fabric, scissors, and a couple of pillow forms to keep me from going stir crazy until I got hired."

Charlene giggled behind her hand. "You remember me from that day?"

"Of course, I do," he said, then squinted, reminding her that he had already admitted he had been 'stalking' her since he'd identified her as one of the two women who had purchased his one-time contribution to a sperm bank that wound up resulting in the birth of two children by two different mothers: Chip by Charlene and Carlos by the now deceased Rosa.

"Yes, I remembered you, but didn't think you remembered me. Did you ever get that pillow cover taken care of? You made quite an impression on me that day. Not only were you willing to take on a 'woman's hobby,' but you wanted to use a quality tool to do it. I didn't think it was just because you were trying to impress me, either."

"The right tool for the right job makes the task less frustrating and more efficient, but I like shiny objects, too," Arlie joked. "Okay now, enough about my desperate attempts at home décor. How about getting out and about and grabbing some snow pants and other cold weather gear? It won't be too long, boys, and you'll be in school!"

"Um..." Charlene interjected.

"Oh, yeah! I'll bet you'd like to know where you'll be going to school, right? How about if we let my friend Marc show us the house he's willing to rent us."

"Is it in Chewbacca town?" Chip asked.

"That's Chew Ghee Ak," Charlene enunciated. "You might as well learn to pronounce it if you're going to be living there."

The boys looked at each other and carefully repeated, "Chew Ghee Ak," with Chip adding an extra 'Ak' to the name.

"We'll work on it. In the meantime, bundle up. Dad will warm up the car..."

Ba room! Arlie waved his keys at her, reminding her he had a remote starter.

"Looks like Dad *is* warming up the car. Let's go find out if we all like Marc's place. Then we can have a home with a yard and you can build a snowman!"

"Like Frosty?" Chip asked.

"Like Frosty, except he won't dance or sing," Arlie said.

"But he'll probably stick around until Easter in that neighborhood," Marc said. "You know where it is, Arlie. I'll meet you out there."

"I still can't place him," Charlene said after Marc was gone. "I'll figure it out, I'm sure."

***

"I want to move here!" Carlos said before Arlie had even shut off the engine.

"What? You haven't even looked inside."

"Yeah, I want to live here, too," Chip said. "See, Dad, it already has a tire swing. You won't have to build one for us. We can take turns, and look! There's a tree fort, too!"

Marc walked up as Arlie opened the Hummer door to let the boys out. "You sabotaged me with the tire swing and tree fort, you know…"

"No, I didn't," Marc answered. "I put those up last summer when I thought I'd have two daughters moving in with me. This place is near a park, so they'll have a safe sledding hill nearby. They'll have to take a bus to school, but that's a lot safer than walking on these roads in the winter. There are plenty of other kids in the neighborhood to play with, too."

"Why are you renting it, Marc?" Charlene asked, as she huddled closer to Arlie.

"Sorry," Marc said as he realized that Charlene was no longer used to Alaska cold. "Let's go inside where it's warmer."

Everyone slipped off shoes, then walked into the sprawling carpeted living room with two leather recliners, a big screen TV, and a nine-piece sectional sofa. "Wow! Does it come furnished, or have you just not had the time to move out your furniture?" Charlene asked.

"What you see is what you're renting, Char. I just got married a month ago. We were thinking of moving here, but my wife's a teacher and wanted to live closer to her school. She already had a house with her two children. We decided it was easier to move me in with her than the other way around. Between a long out-of-town assignment and the holidays, I never got around to selling what I had here. When Abby told me that Arlie was getting married and it was a package deal, well, I decided to wait a month or two before putting this place up for rent or sale. I know Arizona is warm, but there's something about Alaska that keeps pulling you back."

"Even after seven years, I still had the feeling that I was an Alaskan living in Arizona and that I'd make it back here again sometime." Charlene shifted her shoulders as she realized the only reason she hadn't come back sooner was because she was jealous of her father's new wife. She swallowed her discomfort and changed subjects. She opened a kitchen cabinet door. "So, you even supply dishes?" She opened a lower cabinet, "And pots and pans?"

"All I took was my garlic mincer. Dottie didn't have one of those. She's new to being an Italian food *aficionado*."

"And the swing?" Arlie asked.

"I put that up for the girls last summer, then helped them build their dream log cabin. They're a couple years older than your boys, but they'll probably all get along."

Carlos and Chip burst into the kitchen, breathless with excitement. "There's two fireplaces and three bedrooms. That means Carlos and I could have our own bedrooms, but I don't want to sleep alone. Can we still be in the same bedroom?"

Carlos's face was pale with fear at his brother's question. He had shown minimal remorse and no depression after his mother had been killed, but the wide eyes of panic at being separated from his new brother at night was unmistakable.

"Yeah, you guys can share the same room as long as you want. So, Charlene, what do you think?"

She pulled back the curtains to watch the sun through the southern window. "High noon already? Where'd the day go? Yes. This is perfect, especially this window. I can watch the sun rise and set from here during the winter, and it won't be in my face in the summer. All I need to do is make a mega shopping trip to get food, laundry supplies, and a few extra sheets and towels, then we can move in whenever is good for you, Marc." Charlene paused as she realized she hadn't conferred with Arlie. "That is, if it's okay with Arlie and the boys."

"I think they already gave you their answer," Arlie said, "and this is perfect for me, too. I noticed there's already sheets and towels in the hall closet, though."

Marc chuckled, commenting before Charlene had a

chance to make excuses. "I haven't been married that long, Arlie, but one thing I've learned is that women need to pick out their own linens, and no matter how clean a place is, they will insist on vacuuming and scrubbing the floors, right, Char?"

"Right..." Charlene answered. "Remind me to buy a new mop and vacuum, Arlie."

"I'll go see if I can drag the boys away. I'd like to get the shopping done while we still have daylight. Marc, do you want me to sign a lease or something?"

"Nope. I'll write down my bank account and utility numbers. Change over the gas and electric right away, if you don't mind. Deposit the rent money into my checking on the first of the month. You can have the rest of this month free as an engagement present."

Marc reached into his pocket. "One for you, Arlie," he said, handing him a house key, "and one for you, Char."

Char. Why does he keep calling me Char… The only one who ever called me Char was Marco in high school, the greasy-haired geek with the half-inch thick glasses who dominated the debate team.

As soon as Arlie was out of the room, Charlene said,

"Marco."

"Polo. I wondered how long it would take you to remember me," Marc said. "A bit of Lasik surgery and redirection on career choice, and now I'm a US Marshal."

"Well, you would have been a great lawyer, too," Charlene said. "Oh, and your hair looks better short, too."

"The boys want to play in the fort for a while, but I told them they'd have to wait until tomorrow. If we do this right, we only have one more night at the hotel. We missed check out time an hour ago."

"Tsk, tsk." Charlene shook her head at Arlie, squinted her eyes at him, and repeated, *"Tsk, tsk."*

A quick snort of a laugh escaped Marc, then he leaned against the wall and continued laughing. When he finally composed himself, he said, "Oh, man, you're done for, Arlie. She has you by the *tsk, tsks!*"

"Yes, dear. I'm sorry I was being so cheap. Let's go into Eagle River and get what we need, bring it back here, and then either you or I—or all of us—can go back to Anchorage and get what little we have at the hotel and bring it back here. Does that plan sound acceptable?"

"Yes, but I think I may flip you to see who has to go into

Anchorage during drive time traffic and who gets to stay here and check out the comfy chairs and sofas."

"I'll make the long stop-and-go trip, then we'll see who flips whom when I get back!"

***

Carlos hid behind the circular display of snowsuits and jackets, then beelined to hide under Arlie's arm. "What's wrong, buddy?"

"I just saw him, and I didn't want him to see me. He's gone now." Carlos peeked out from around Arlie, then returned to his secreted position, not saying a word.

The hairs rose on the back of Arlie's neck, whether from the fear his young son was transmitting with his panicked clutching or from cop's second nature. He didn't know what to do yet, but he knew to stay cool for right now. "We're okay, but we'll stay put, just in case."

Arlie pivoted in place, a feigned shopper's frown on his face as he looked towards the displays, bypassing the contents and looking beyond them to the shoppers. Someone in the store had frightened Carlos.

And there he was. Lucky De Luca. The twenty-something-year-old small-time crook claimed to be Alonzo

117

De Luca's illegitimate son, but no one on the force believed the urban legend. The man's hair was definitely dyed coal black to match the swarthy Italian family's, but there was nothing he could do about his lithe and wiry frame, nothing like the De Luca men's thick bulky bodies. The cocky young man also blinked constantly, like he was wearing contact lenses that hadn't been changed in months.

Lucky looked around, then—satisfied that the coast was clear—stuffed a camo-print wallet from the shelf into the inside pocket of his black down-filled jacket. Arlie turned away, but continued to view the petty thief in the reflection of the mirror near the hat display as he pocketed a cheap sport watch.

"What's going on?" Charlene asked as she and Chip walked up to a scared Carlos and intent Arlie.

Arlie flinched at her voice, but didn't change his stance. He pasted on a fake smile and turned to her as if nothing had happened. "Oh, it looks like an almost cousin of Carlos has shown up."

"He's supposed to be my brother," Carlos said, then turned his head and blew a dry raspberry. "Lucky said he was the real heir to Alonzo De Luca's business, not me. He used to pull my hair and call me a ginger bastard. My mom—my other mom—caught him doing it once. I don't know what she did or said to him, but he squealed like a baby and never came near me again."

Arlie felt his stomach knot up, bile squirting into the back of his throat. *Ginger Bastard!* Was it just a crass remark about the boy's red hair, or did the De Lucas know about his youth as a passed-around foster care child without a father?

"Your first mother was a great woman. I'm glad she protected you from gutter rats like Lucky and the others. She's not here, but you do know we'll take care of you and won't let him or any of the other De Lucas near you, right?"

Carlos nodded his head. "I'm sorta glad that, that," he whispered the name, "Alonzo," then spoke up again, "never let Mama give me the name De Luca. She told me, 'You're just Carlos, so great that you don't need a second name.' But I'm glad I'm a Biggar now. I like that name."

"I'm glad, too," Arlie said, then turned to Charlene. "I don't know what's going on here. I thought the whole family moved Outside years ago, that Alonzo and his brother just popped in six months ago to get that hard drive. I sort of got in their way. They didn't know I could listen in on their calls."

"So, if you had his phone number right now, you could hear who he's talking to and what he's saying?" Charlene asked.

Before he could answer, Carlos tugged on his sleeve. "Daddy, I gotta go pee."

"Just a min…"

"Really, really bad," Carlos said, his eyes misty, his hands clutching his crotch.

That jerk probably scared the piss right out of him. Take care of family first, dude!

"Sure, let's go. Come on, Chip. We might as well empty all the water buckets at the same time."

"Huh?"

"Let's all go pee at the same time," Carlos whispered.

"Oh. Okay. I'm sure glad I get to go in the men's room, now. It's great to have a daddy!"

***

Charlene rushed up to Arlie from behind the shelves just outside of the restrooms. "I got the phone number for you, Arlie," she said, giddy and bouncy, unable to contain her excitement.

"What?" Arlie screeched in a hoarse whisper, his eyes

wide with rage.

"Slow down there, big boy. You're not the only one with skills, you know," she said with a sly grin, flipping her hair back in a suggestive way.

"How. Did. You. Get. It?" he asked, teeth clenched.

"Daddy, you're hurting my hand," Carlos said, trying to wrench his hand out of Arlie's tight grip.

"I just went up to him, asked him if he was the hot guy I met at Cicero's last weekend because if he was, I lost his phone number and I'd really like to hook up."

"Jesus Christ, woman! What were you thinking?"

"Are you and Mommy fighting?" Chip asked. "Cause if you are, you're scaring Carlos. And me, too, a little."

Arlie took a deep, steadying breath. "No, we're not fighting. I'm just trying to find out what she said and to whom and why. She scared me. Sometimes people's voices get loud when they're scared and I'm real scared."

Charlene thrust the contest entry form with the name 'Lucky' and a phone number written on the back at Arlie's chest, not even aiming for his hand. "You're welcome," she huffed. "Come on, boys. Let's go pick up some new sheets for your beds. I'll bet you've never slept on flannel before, have you, Carlos?"

As his family walked away, safe in the wide aisles of the department store, Arlie took out his smartphone. He swiped the screen and held it up to his face, as if looking for something on the screen. His coy move initiated the facial recognition scan and unlocked the surveillance app he had created two months earlier. He keyed in the phone number Charlene had given him, verifying that it was the same one he had 'snatched' with another app when he first recognized Lucky. The GPS blip popped up, an eerie purple tone he had assigned as a potentially dangerous contact. He watched the post-Christmas bargain hunters mill around, glancing down casually as his space-age divining rod locked into Lucky's phone location, using both its carrier's MSIN and phone number to find him.

A sigh of relief escaped when he had the full menu of Lucky's phone options. Now he could listen in on the imbecile's calls, read his texts in real time, and search both the phone's built in and removable memories. Arlie double-tapped the corner of his screen to upload Lucky's phone history and memory card content to his secure cloud account, then allowed a grin to emerge. Removing what looked like a Band Aid packet from his pocket, he slapped the wrapper's mottled black logo on the concentric swirl icon on his phone, synching the micro ear piece to his phone. Biting the edge of the packet, he tore it apart, removed the little flesh-toned pellet, and stuck it behind his ear. His custom created 'bionic mole' would enable him to listen in on every incoming and outgoing phone call Lucky made.

Hopefully Lucky didn't live up to the name he had given himself. Lucky that while everyone else in the family had been sent to jail, he had 'lucked out' and was a free man.

***

Bzzz. And there it was. Lucky was already calling out. Arlie walked over to the display of scarves, mindlessly pawing through the colorful woven neck pieces as he concentrated on the call.

Click. The connection was made, but no one had so much as said hello.

"Hey, G. I know I'm not supposed to call," Lucky said, showing his nervousness by the even higher pitch of his voice, "but I just got doused with more of my good luck. You won't believe it, but remember that creepy red-headed cop who wouldn't take a bribe?"

"Uh huh."

"I'll take that as a yes. Well, anyhow, I think his girlfriend has the hots for me. I mean, this fine piece of woman walks up to me, asks me for my number—again—and then she takes off. I watched her go back to the bathrooms and then, wham! She's kissing on him! That Charles Baggar has a real slut for a girlfriend."

"Uhh..."

"Yeah, I know. I'll see if I can hang out with her long enough to find out where he's hanging. I thought he was going to stay in Arizona after he put Dad and Uncle Luca in jail. I didn't see that brat Carlos around, so maybe he got tired of him and ditched him down there. I mean, I know that's one of the reasons Dad went down there—to clean up the garbage—but let Arizona have the kid. I just don't want that bastard around here."

"Uh huh!"

"Well, it's been nice talking to you, G. Oh, and his hair's still long. I'll call when I've got his scalp ready for your collection."

"Heh, heh, heh."

"'Til then."

Click.

Arlie's stomach pinched so tight, it felt as if it was being squeezed up his throat, like toothpaste from a near empty tube. He swallowed hard to force it back down, then concentrated on his phone, throwing up digital blockades to confine the creep, keep him from reaching out again. Swiping across the screen twice blocked any new outgoing phone calls or texts, isolating Lucky from calling for help from comrades, but would still allow incoming—and hopefully, intimidating calls and texts—to be received. It was time to dam up Lucky De Luca's flow of good luck.

Now he needed to find out who this new player 'G' was. There was no way to obtain a voice recognition analysis on grunts or evil laughs. He couldn't even tell if it was a man or a woman Lucky had called. No caller ID number showed up on his app, either. Maybe he had tagged into the call too late. The click he had heard was probably from a relay, not the actual phone number Lucky had dialed.

None of this made any difference right now, though. Lucky's stated number one priority was to pursue Charlene in order to get to him. He'd have to run interference to keep him away from her right now.

"What are you doing, Arlie? I'd tease you about picking out a pretty scarf to go with your new cocktail dress, but now that you have Char in your life, you have an excuse for checking out the pretties."

"Sometimes you have to make your own good luck," Arlie said to himself, and slid his phone into his pocket. *You're not a single man anymore, dude. You have a family to think about now. No jumping into the middle of a take down when the dominoes look right. You have them to consider.*

"Are you okay, Arlie?" Marc asked, bumping shoulders with him to get his attention. "You're as white a polar bear's ass."

Arlie shook his head, trying to figure out if he should or shouldn't jump in blindly. He had to act fast. No time to build a team or even tell Cap what he was up to. Charlene was tough and could handle the transition to a new home in a new state with two kindergarteners. It was a lot to dump on her, but he was desperate. It was better to ask forgiveness than permission... And if he didn't do something right now—before Lucky reached out to more contacts—she might not be around for him to ask anything!

"Crap! Marc, I have to do this," Arlie said, his mind made

up.

"Do what? Move into my house? I'm fine with it, and so are Charlene and the boys. Great family, by the way."

"No, not that. I gotta do this right now. Help out Charlene and the boys, would ya? Tell her I love her and I'm doing this for all of us. Lucky's onto Charlene and is going after her. I have to stop him. Abby will know where I am, sorta, and if I'm dead or alive. I'll call you when it's safe. Until then, you and Cap will have to trust me."

Marc squinted, checking for any signs of hesitation. Nope. None. Arlie was going to do this whether it was sanctioned or not. Whether he lost his job or not. Hopefully, he knew what he was getting into and would follow it through. If not, he'd be lucky if he only lost his job. Worst case scenario, he'd lose his life, leaving two orphans and a widow before he even had a chance to get married.

Marc sighed and shook his head. "There's no changing your mind, is there?"

"Nope." Arlie fist-bumped Marc's shoulder. "This is a speed of light mission. Let's hope all I am is late for dinner."

"I've got your back," Marc said. "Just don't turn it on anyone."

"I did once and have the scar to prove it. It won't happen again."

"It was twice, but who's counting."

Arlie thrust his car keys at Marc. "Take care of them. Please."

Marc watched as his sometime joint venture partner weaved through the clearance racks and out the front door. He saw Arlie pause a moment, then jump in front of a modified black Jeep, slapping his hand down on the hood of the car.

"It's a crosswalk, jackass!" he hollered, then ran around to the passenger door. Words were spoken through the opened window, and then Arlie climbed into the front seat of the ebony and chrome lifted four-wheel-drive vehicle, a cocky smile pasted on his face that Marc hoped meant that this would be a quick bust and Arlie would only be late for supper.

And not another scalped agent found at the edge of the Matanuska River.

Chapter 7
Walking

In 2015, 5,376 people were killed in pedestrian/motor vehicle crashes, nearly 15 people every day of the year (NHTSA Traffic Safety Facts). This represents the highest number of pedestrians killed in one year since 1996. Though total traffic fatalities in the US fell by nearly 18 percent from 2006 to 2015, pedestrian fatalities rose by 12 percent during the same ten-year period. (https://crashstats.nhtsa.dot.gov/Api/Public/ViewPublication/8 12375)

Thump! Thump!

Arlie smacked the hood of wide-eyed Lucky's pimped ride, shouted, "It's a crosswalk, jackass," then ran around the front of the shiny midnight and chrome lifted Jeep with tires the size of black bears. He grabbed the side mirror brace, opened the door, and slid into the burgundy tuck-and-roll upholstered passenger seat.

"Well, if it isn't Lucky De Luca," he said, then reached around and pulled out the seatbelt and buckled in.

Lucky's mouth hung open in shock, his hand limp on the gear shift knob.

"Come on, let's go get something to eat," Arlie said, then put his hand on top of Lucky's, moving the transmission into first gear. "I'm starved. Oh, and you're buying."

"Wha…What are you doing here?" the stunned faux-brunette asked as he released the clutch and took his foot off the brake, ready to roll.

"I saw you in the store. I thought it might be a good chance to re-connect. I hate to say it, but times are tough. I thought maybe you and I could transact some business. Maybe some of your luck will rub off on me." Arlie arched his back and winced, as if in pain. "Life's been upside down for me for the last six months or so. I think it's time to change my loyalties."

Lucky's eyes cut over to Arlie, unsure if he was being punked or if he was having a flashback from the mushrooms he sampled the night before. "Where to for dinner?"

"How about that little Chinese place over in Spenard? It should be discreet. That is, unless you don't want to drive that far…"

"No, no, I'm fine. They have pretty good lo mein. So, what brings you out here, Daywalker?" Lucky asked. "Last I heard, you were in Arizona, causing havoc for my dad and uncle."

Wow! He doesn't beat around the bush or know how to play tickle!

"Sorry, but your old man didn't give me much choice. I was trying to get into the pants of a sweet brunette hottie. She latched on to me 'cause she said I made her juicy and tingly all over. Something about how I looked like her bastard son." Arlie grimaced and twisted his back again, continuing the ruse of still having a bullet in his back. *It's tough, dude, but you have to think of Charlene as a manipulative bimbo. Hide your true feelings!*

"Anyhow, all was looking great until the boy latched onto another red-headed kid and they started hanging out together. Shit! Then I had to contend with two brats while trying to make my moves on her. I was all set to drop the boys off at the mall after taking them to, ugh, a park, when your old man and Luca came out with guns and fists. Shit! I had to make myself look like the good guy, protecting her little brat. That was sure to get me at least one trip around the world with her! Turns out, I grabbed the wrong kid. All that cactus, a bullet, and I still got blue balls!"

Lucky's mouth twisted into a near smile, then he frowned

again, waiting for more of the story.

"Yeah, and then I follow her all the way up here, and what does she do? She starts bar hopping! I've caught her hanging all over two other guys in less than a week! I'm done with her and that brat. All she wanted was a sugar daddy. I'm nobody's daddy! She has some expensive habits, too. My bank accounts are zapped. If I don't walk away from her now, while I still have some dignity, she'll be walking away from me first." Arlie grunted, then reached up and rubbed the stubble on his chin. "Come to think of it, she already has walked out on me. Two other guys in less than a week!"

"Three," Lucky said. "She hit on me in the store, said she lost my phone number." Lucky revved the engine and changed lanes, his back tires spinning on the black ice the other drivers had slowed down to avoid.

Arlie's butt cheeks clenched at the erratic driving. He changed his dash-grabbing move into repositioning himself into a more comfortable position, and tried to look relaxed. "Women! You can't live with 'em, and you can't shoot 'sem."

"Speak for yourself," Lucky said, then laughed, paused, then laughed even louder and longer.

What did you get yourself into, dude! He's crazy!

Or he's testing you…

"So," Arlie said, intentionally changing the subject, "the reason I wanted to catch up with you is I'm looking for a job. I don't know who's taken over the family business now that Alonzo and Luca are warming their hides in the Valley of the Sun, but I figured you'd know. I need to build up my cash reserves again. I figure with a few of the right jobs, I can retire to somewhere in South or Central America where they speak English."

"Costa Rica is a great place," Lucky said, then looked over his shoulder, ready to make another hurry-up lane change. "I knew a gal who lived there for quite a while. She was okay, but she's, ahem, gone now."

Rosa! Carlos's mother, God rest her soul. It doesn't sound like he was in on it, though. He almost sounds as if he's sad about it. File that away for future use.

The Jeep veered right and tipped on its side, suddenly on two wheels. Arlie leaned across Lucky and clutched both sides of the thin man's seat to shift his weight to the airborne side, hoping it would be enough to bring all four wheels back down to the road surface.

Thunk!

It worked.

"Yup, they call you Lucky for a reason," Arlie said. "Now, about a job…"

"Word is that you're friendly with a few of the judges on the bench," Lucky replied. "One of those has never been too friendly to family businesses, so it's time for him to retire. Or resign. Or disappear. G doesn't care which one, as long as he's gone."

G! Who in the hell is G? Don't ask or he'll know you're fishing.

"You know, I'm actually pretty sharp," Arlie said, "But I don't recall *any* of the judges being friendly with family businesses. You're going to have to give me a name. Oh, and of course, a number. I don't work for free."

"It's the tall judge. Taylor," Lucky said dryly.

"So, why don't you do it?" Arlie asked. "I mean, is there something tough about the job or do you have a personal fondness for the guy, or maybe there's not enough money in it for you…"

Lucky looked over at him, the oncoming headlights casting an eerie glow over his face before it disappeared into the darkness of the Jeep's interior. "I have my reasons," he said, then didn't make another sound until they pulled up to their dinner destination.

The restaurant was tucked into the back corner of a poorly plowed and dimly lit parking lot, gritty-gray snow piles heaped two-cars high and three times as long on all perimeters, making the red pagoda-shaped edifice look like a smushed cherry in an oversized cup of marshmallow cocoa. Lucky gunned the engine and Arlie saw his intent.

"Could you at least drop me off at the front door before you try to park on top of Mount Denali?" he asked, nodding to the huge snow dump in front of them. "Give a poor cripple a break," he added, rubbing his lower back.

Lucky chuckled, then put the Jeep in reverse and spun away from the huge snow pile, his fast turnaround braking to a stop in a handicapped parking place. "I guess I can cut you some slack. Better?" he asked.

"Yeah, thanks. Do you come here often?"

Lucky walked in front of Arlie and smacked the door open with a quick shove and a thud that sent the little brass bells tied to the handle screeching against the plate glass, the metallic jingles of the clappers adding to a cacophony even a deaf dog could hear.

"Ah, Mr. Lucky," the matronly Asian hostess said in greeting, then bowed deeply and handed him a menu. "I see you brought a friend tonight." She handed Arlie a menu. "Your usual place in the back?"

"Hmph! I guess that answers that," Arlie said, although he had suggested the place because he already knew it was a known hang out for the De Lucas. He sat down and glanced over the menu, unable to concentrate on the dozens of rice and noodle dishes listed in front of him, his mind spinning in a completely different world. "Well, what do you suggest?" he asked to make conversation. "You say they have good lo mein?"

How in the hell did you think you'd get Lucky to bring you into the inner sanctum of the De Luca gang? Do you have brain damage? Plant the seed, let him know you're interested, then get out and develop a strategy that includes back up! What kind of superhero do you think you are?

"Lo mein, high mein, everything's good here." Lucky closed his eyes, flipped the menu around a few times, opened it up, and stabbed a spot with his index finger. "Hmm. Looks like it's pork fried rice for me tonight? How about you?"

Arlie copied Lucky's move, but used his thumb to choose

his dish. "Happy family? What in the heck is that? How about if I just have pork fried rice, too. I know I like that. Oh, and I'll have a cup of hot and sour soup, too." He brushed his hands up and down the outside of his arms, warming up his goosebumps of fear and insecurity. "Damn, it's cold tonight!"

"You want hot and sour soup, too, Mr. Lucky?" the same matronly woman asked.

"Yeah, that sounds good," Lucky said, eyeing Arlie as if he was trying to remember something. "Real good."

"So," Arlie said, then looked up in the mirror behind Lucky's head, watching the patrons. "You gave me a name, but not a number or time frame. Any other specifics? Is it supposed to look like an accident? Do you want me to frame someone else?"

Lucky lowered his head and stared into Arlie's eyes. "Let's make this perfectly clear, it's not *me* who wants anything done. It's a family deal. Right now, until I'm graciously acknowledged by Papa De Luca, I'm not *real* family. I'm just a courier. A messenger. Got it?"

"Whoa, there fella," Arlie said, glad the room was dim, so Lucky couldn't see the sweat on his upper lip or his eyes dilated in fear. Instead, he made light of Lucky's cold proclamation. "I'm just looking for a job, man. I don't care if you're the one paying me or you're just a fur and flesh courier pigeon. I have skills. I can make it look like the old guy slipped in the shower if that's what Papa or whoever wants." He shifted in his seat, feigning discomfort as he tried to figure out a quick way to grab information then split. "We still haven't talked numbers. I don't care how much you get for running interference, either, if my piece of the pie is enough to take care of me for a while. A federal judge isn't like knocking off the dealer down the street who's skimming. This comes with a lot of liability. As a cop—even one on disability leave—I could get life if I'm caught."

"Then don't get caught," Lucky said, then slurped the soup the young waitress had brought to him. "Ah, just right..." He set the cup down, then his face fell.

Arlie looked in the mirror behind his erstwhile patron and saw what Lucky had seen.

Gordo.

The big Italian was definitely a De Luca. Even Alonzo and Luca backed away when their surly nephew entered the room. He was about the same age as Lucky, but that's where the similarity ended. Gordo was at least 6'5" and maybe four hundred pounds. Whether his bulk was muscle or fat didn't make a difference. Arlie had followed up with some of his victims in the hospital. He was ruthless. He had been a suspect in a string of assaults and murders in the homeless community, but no one would testify against him. Because of his reputation, he was untouchable.

"Good evening, Mr. De Luca," the middle-aged Asian hostess said. "We have your order ready in a minute."

Gordo grumbled, but didn't say a word.

Arlie and Lucky listened to the high-pitched chatter of the staff in the back as they hollered at each other in their Asian dialect, cutlery clanging to the floor and paper rustling, as they hurried to finalize his order.

Thirty seconds later, the man who must be chef by the looks of his apron, came out. "We hope you like," he said, and gave a short bow to Gordo. "Your total is $112 tonight."

Gordo pulled a fat wad of bills out of his pocked and peeled off a hundred-dollar bill. "Here," he said, and reached for the bag.

"No, no. Sorry, but it is $112 tonight. You have eight dinners, not seven."

The big man looked in the bag. "No napkins? I need

some napkins," he demanded.

Arlie and Lucky watched as the waitress who had brought them their soup grabbed a fistful of paper napkins, spat quickly into the bundle, then said, "I have your napkins here, mister."

She rushed over and placed the napkins in the bag, then grabbed a handful of cellophane-wrapped fortune cookies from the dispenser next to the cash register. "You have good fortune tonight, too, mister," then bowed and rushed into the kitchen.

Lucky and Arlie looked at each other, each of them stifling a chuckle.

"My order's still late, so there's a penalty," Gordo said, and threw the hundred-dollar bill at the chef. He grabbed the container of cookies and dumped it into his paper sack of take-out food, emptying all of them into it, then tossed it back on the counter. "And it better be good," he sneered, then straight-armed the door open into the winter cold, cramming the aluminum-framed glass into the snow pile behind it.

The chef ran after him, shouting in his native language, shaking his fist, then came back, frowning as he pulled the door shut behind him.

"It's a good thing Gordo likes the food here," Lucky said. "Otherwise, he wouldn't put up with the old man's cussing, whether he understands what he's saying or not." He set his cup down. "I think I've lost my appetite. Let's go."

The two men went to the counter. Lucky pulled out a hundred-dollar bill and handed it to the hostess who had seated them. "Sorry, but something just came up, so we won't be eating. Thanks for the soup." He rolled his eyes at her and canted his head toward the door. "And sorry about him, too."

"You good man, Mr. Lucky," she said. "You come back later. I make you something special. You too skinny."

"I'll do that," Lucky said, then turned to Arlie. "Let's go talk business."

So much for grabbing information then making a quick getaway!

Chapter 8
Northern Lights

Aurora: the bright, dancing green tints sometimes seen fluttering and dancing across northern nighttime skies are electrically charged particles from the sun, colliding with earth's gaseous atmosphere as they enter near the magnetic poles, the area where the magnetic fields are weaker and less likely to deflect the solar-spewn particles. These displays are known as Aurora borealis (Northern Lights) in the north and Aurora australis in the southern hemisphere. Auroral displays are usually shades of green and pink, but shades of yellow, blue, and violet have also been reported. Sometimes, the aurora noise—a crackling, hissing sound—can be heard during cold nights when the charged particles from the solar winds hit a frigid inversion layer. Alaska and western Canada are great places to watch the Northern Lights. Southern auroras are less likely to be viewed as they are usually over Antarctica and the southern Indian Ocean.

"Where to now?" Arlie asked, a chill running up his spine despite the Jeep's heated seat.

Lucky laughed, happy to be in charge of a situation for once, looked over at Arlie and winked. "You'll see."

Note to self: Never, ever take off on your own without a

team or a plan again! That is, if you ever get out of this debacle alive!

As soon as they passed the city lights, Lucky started driving like he was on a timed obstacle course, all four tires off the ground at once as he sped over frost heave bumps, landing hard, skidding into icy curves, gaining intermittent control with down shifting and white-knuckled hand-over-hand steering.

Arlie clutched the armrest at his right, his outstretched left arm braced against the dash in front of him. "Are you afraid your ride is going to turn into a pumpkin or something if you don't get home in time?"

"I'm not taking you to my place, Daywalker," Lucky said, then slowed down and turned off his lights. He rolled into the parking lot of the lookout point, squinting into the darkness to make sure they were the only ones around.

Gulp! At least you still have your knife. Let's hope he's just looking for a quiet place to chat and not a dark place to dump a body!

"You *can* drive a stick shift, right?" Lucky asked, a sly smile overtaking his look of indecision.

"A manual transmission? Yeah, three, four, five, or six-speed. Why?"

Lucky reached across Arlie and smacked the front of the glove box with the side of his fist. It popped opened, revealing a large bag of chocolate candies.

"Because I'm gonna take a little trip and you're going to be my driver…in case I need one. You never know what you're getting when you buy botanicals." Lucky pulled open the reclosable yellow plastic pouch, but instead of chocolate-coated peanuts, he pulled out a fistful of brown and tan crumpled bits.

"Want some?" Lucky asked, showing off his handful of psilocybin mushrooms. "Not!" he joked, then shoved all the pieces in his mouth, licking his hand to get the last bits. "You might have to drive later. Don't want you grinding down all my gears or burning up my clutch if you're high."

"Are you eating magic mushrooms?" Arlie asked.

"Give the cop an A for knowing his Schedule One drugs." Lucky tipped the bag into his mouth, sticking his tongue in to get the last crumbs. "I sampled these last night. Not bad, but I just got a taste. Let's see if I can solve at least half the world's problems tonight."

Cool! You may have just received a free ride on the

information highway, dude, and a safe exit to Charlene and the boys. If Lucky is going to be stoned out of his coconut, you just might get more intel from him than if you had a whole game room full of unsanctioned interrogation equipment.

"Wow! Look at those northern lights," Lucky said. "You don't need to be high to appreciate those colors. God, I hope they're still out when these shrooms kick in. I heard you can see a whole new level of greens and purples... Wow..."

Lucky tumbled out of the driver's seat, leaving his keys dangling from the ignition. Arlie grabbed the three-key bundle with a micro-utility tool attached and shoved it in his pocket, then followed the swaying lithe form to the edge of the trees.

"The Coastal Trail," Lucky said. "Have you ever ridden it?"

"Nope. Never had the time. Come to think of it, never had a bike, either."

"Shit, you can rent a bike." Lucky turned back from his view of Cook Inlet and the Coastal Trail that ran beside it, and canted his head as he stared at his tricked-out Jeep, deep in thought.

"Oh, no. You are *not* going to drive that rig down the

slope to the trail." Arlie rubbed his outer arms as a chill ran up them, then remembered he hadn't flinched in pain lately. "Come on. We didn't eat, and I need to take a pain pill or four. Let's find a drive-through. I'm Jones-ing for some chili cheese fries. How about you?"

"Nah, I feel like an adventure!" Lucky exclaimed, and started twirling in a tight but clumsy circle, like an ice dancer in hiking boots, his arms wide to embrace his long-awaited trip into oblivion.

"Well, I don't think there's a way around that! Even if we don't leave this parking lot, you're going to la la land pretty soon. Before you're too far gone, though, how much of that crap did you eat?"

Lucky held up his index finger, then kept adding digits until he was wiggling all five of them.

"Five? You ingested five grams of magic mushrooms?" Arlie asked.

"Well, yeah! I'd get sick if it was five ounces. Besides, I'd need about a fifth of tequila to wash that much down. Speaking of tequila, how about if we get some?"

Arlie saw his opportunity and took it. "That sounds like a great plan to me. Go ahead and climb in. I'll drive us to your place and fix you a drink." *Yeah, right! A drink of ipecac syrup!*

"I don't have any tequila," Lucky said with an exaggerated pout. "Or limes…"

"That's not a problem. I have the keys and I'll take care of you. That's my job tonight, right?"

"Oh, shit… That's not what I'm supposed to do with you. Hey, we've got company!" Lucky ducked, as if someone had just thrown a punch. "I think we better get the hell out of here. Pronto!"

Arlie caught Lucky as he stumbled just before reaching the truck. "Here, let me help. Put your foot on this step," he said, guiding the delusional man who was now swatting at invisible flies.

"That's a sissy bar," Lucky hissed, then lifted his leg high to bypass it, trying and missing the floorboard twice before letting Arlie shoulder him up bodily.

"Well, I guess I'm a sissy tonight, huh, Daywalker?" he asked as Arlie belted him in.

Arlie rushed around the Jeep, jumped in, and started it before answering. "No, you're not a sissy tonight. You're stoned. But don't worry. I'll take care of you."

Arlie looked up. *Great! A GPS! Now let's see if he... All right! Just about everyone programs his home address into the GPS home icon.*

"Are you sure this is where you live?" Arlie asked the still babbling Lucky as he neared the address shown. "We're in the commercial district by the port."

"Yup, my apartment's around back of that big tire warehouse. The path gets a little icy... Oh, look!" Lucky set his chin on the dash and pointed up. "I see a new color of purple! I think I'll call it Cold Weenie Purple!"

"Ah, well, that's a good description, all right, but I doubt if they'll use that name for kids' crayons." Arlie walked around and opened the Jeep door for Lucky. "Come on, let me help you get situated inside. Remember, you left me in charge."

"Yes, sir!" Lucky said, and raised his arm in salute just as his feet hit the ground. "Oh, I shouldn't have done that. You're the bad guy and I'm the good guy. I'm supposed to be setting you up for..."

Lucky's words stopped as he collapsed into a mound of polar fleece and nylon at Arlie's feet. "Well, let's hope it isn't too far around back," Arlie mumbled as he pulled the incoherent man to his wobbly feet. "You're getting a fireman's carry tonight, buddy. And yes, you're lucky my back isn't screwed up anymore or I'd have left you where you fell and brought you inside with a wheelbarrow."

The cocoa fiber mat at the back door read, 'Go Away.' *Must be his place.* "Is this your home, Lucky?"

"Huh? Oh, you found it. Not very fancy, but when I bring you into Papa, he'll move me up and then I'll have a real nice layout…"

Arlie used the only housekey on the keyring to unlock the dented gunmetal gray door.

First things first. Make sure he doesn't puke and choke on his own vomit. There! That recliner should keep him upright. Now, what does he have in his medicine cabinet? Syrup of ipecac? Nope. Hemorrhoid cream? Really? Hmm. Not much more than ibuprofen and cotton swabs. Either he's a lightweight, or he has his heavy-duty consumables somewhere else. Maybe there's something in the kitchen…

"Where's my tequila?" Lucky hollered, then added in a sing song voice, "One tequila, two tequila, three tequila…"

"Floor!" Arlie hollered back. "Hold tight. I'm mixing a drink for you right now."

Arlie turned on the hot water tap while he searched for a

clean glass and the salt. He settled for a quickly rinsed out coffee cup, added a couple tablespoons of salt, hot water, and stirred, making a strong and simple emetic. "And that's what they sent me to first aid class for," he said softly.

"Here you go, Lucky," Arlie said, and pulled the barroom ballad singing rag doll forward. "I might have put a bit too much salt on the rim, but don't worry about it. It'll do its stuff in no time."

"You forgot the lime," Lucky said with a mope.

"You're not a sissy tonight, Lucky. Straight tequila, with just a little salt on the rim. Prove you're as big a man as Papa."

That did it. Lucky's back straightened up at the challenge. "I'm twice the man he or Alonzo or Luca or any of those other *legitimate* De Lucas are!" He guzzled half the cup before he tasted it, gagged slightly, then polished off the rest with a mouth-swiping flourish. "Ah! I'll have another."

"No, I think one ought to do it," Arlie said, almost feeling guilty. He plopped down on an upside-down bucket and leaned forward, pulled his smartphone from his inner jacket pocket, and set it to record. "Now, I have a few questions I want to ask you. First off, what's your name, Lucky."

"Lucky De Luca. My mother put Luis De Luca on my birth certificate," he said plainly, then boasted, "But I'm Lucky De Luca!"

"All right, Lucky. Earlier this evening, you and I were talking about a job to get rid of Judge Taylor. Who wants the hit?"

"Papa De Luca. He wants him gone, but he has an even bigger bounty out on The Daywalker. That's you, Charles Baggar. You put two of his sons in jail. And you also stopped him from cleaning up the family name."

"How did I do that?"

Suddenly, Lucky's spirited responses were gone, and he was sobbing like he had just run over his puppy with a lawnmower.

"Lucky," Arlie said, squatted down next to him, genuinely concerned. "What's wrong?"

"They killed her! I tried and I tried to get her to stay gone, but they found her and killed her?"

"Who?" Arlie asked, biting off the name 'Rosa.' Lucky had to say it, not just agree to it.

"Rosa. I loved her. She didn't love me, but I loved her even if she thought I was being mean to Carlos when I pinched him. Is it hot in here? I'm hot." Lucky pulled his long-sleeved tee shirt off over his head.

"Okay, I understand you loved Rosa, even if she was married to Alonzo. She was a beautiful woman and wonderful mother. Now tell me, how did I keep Papa from cleaning up the family name?"

"You stopped him from finishing the job in Arizona. He said Rosa was a slut and her kid was a bastard. The boy's red hair was an insult to both Alonzo and to the family name," Lucky reached up and ran his fingers through his hair, moving it out of his face. He sighed, "And they both had to go." Lucky nodded to Arlie. "He didn't like it that you saved Carlos. Even if Papa never let the kid have the De Luca name, the boy was still the son of his daughter-in-law and followed her everywhere, like a shadow at her heels. The boy's constant presence pissed him off."

"Wait. You said she thought you were being mean when you pinched Carlos. Why would you pinch him?"

"Alonzo would have me and one of his goons sneak up on the kid, setting him up to tumble down a flight of stairs or fall off a balcony. I'd say mean things to him, then pinch him so he'd call out for his Mama. I guess you could say I was giving him some of my luck." Lucky wiped his nose with his shirt and sniffed a couple times before tossing it into the corner. "She thought I was hurting Carlos, but I was really saving him."

And then Arlie noticed it. He turned on the lamp next to the recliner. "Lucky, reach up for just a minute."

"Why?"

"Simon says reach to the sky," Arlie said.

Reflexively, Lucky's arms shot up. "One arm or two."

"Simon says relax."

Man, oh, man! Lucky's armpit hair is red! I never thought too much about his pale complexion—maybe it was poor nutrition—but it's typical of red heads, too. If he lived anywhere but Alaska, he would probably freckle. Contact lenses let him have brown eyes like the rest of the De Lucas. He remembered to color his eyebrows when he dyed his hair, but it looked like Lucky didn't think about his underarm hair.

"How long have you known Alonzo was not your daddy?" Arlie asked, switching from friend to interrogator mode. "Did your mama tell you with her dying breath?"

Lucky squirmed, trying to keep the tears at bay. After he had found her blood-soaked body, he had cried for two months solid. He thought he had run out of tears, but now they were forming again.

"I'll bet a hundred bucks you didn't know Alonzo was the one who put the hit on your mama—his former girlfriend and the first love of his life—did you?"

Squoosh! There was no actual sound, but Arlie watched as Lucky deflated, as if all air, energy, and substance had been sucked from his body. Not even a wet tear was left. He was nothing more than an empty bony shell, ashy white, slumped over with sorrow and humiliation.

"I was pretty sure you didn't know, but you just confirmed it. If it makes you feel any better, I just found out about it, too. You probably already knew that Carlos wasn't his kid, either. The boy didn't look any more like him than you, although you went out of your way to try to emulate him in both looks and dirty deeds."

Lucky reached up and plucked out his brown-tinted contact lenses and flipped them away, like he was flicking boogers off his fingertips. "I didn't do his dirty deeds, but I didn't speak up, either. Does that make me a bad man?" he whined, his elbows pulled together in cowardly shame. He started rocking back and forth, reverting to a childlike state, either from humiliation or from his psychedelic mushroom experience or both.

"Lucky," Arlie said, pulling the scared man-child's face up to look him in the eye, "Alonzo tried to kill little five-year-old Carlos last month just because he wasn't his blood. What do you think he'll have Papa do to you when he finds out that you've been deceiving him all your life, that the only reason there's any resemblance between the two of you is because of Lady Clairol and Bausch and Lomb? Those were colored contacts you just tossed away, right?"

Lucky froze, then nodded. Stoned or sober, he didn't have anything to say.

"Don't you think he might have been a bit curious as to why his little boy's blue eyes suddenly turned dark-brown, Lucky? Your mother was wise to never leave you alone with him, only letting the three of you meet in darkened restaurants with low light and lots of hustle and bustle around. She saved your life by being clever. Too bad you weren't clever enough to save hers."

"But, but..."

Slam!

The one and only door to the small ground floor

apartment flung open, startling the two men deep in discussion in the middle of the room. Lucky pulled his knees to his chest in fear, gripping himself in a tight knot, his face buried into his chest.

"Shit!" Arlie jumped up and grabbed the knife from his ankle sheath, then moved in front of the overstuffed chair that held his stoned and quivering interrogatee, ready to protect the incapacitated squealer if needed.

"Having a little party, Lucky?" the dark-haired man filling the doorway asked.

Gordo stepped inside and slammed the door behind him, never taking his eyes from the two. "When you called in earlier, I thought you were bringing in someone for me to toy with. Looks to me like someone's been toying with you instead. Word on the street was you played for both teams, but I never thought you'd spread 'em for a cop."

"Leave him alone," Arlie said.

"Whoa! Big bad Anchorage dick protecting his little boyfriend, eh?" Gordo laughed at his own joke. "Anchorage dick as in detective as in you want to dick my little cousin," he said, then laughed again, even louder.

"What do you want, Gordo," Arlie asked, glancing at his

phone, then at the window, the only escape route other than the front door. The phone was still recording, but he hadn't set it up to share the information with anyone. If he hadn't gone off half-cocked, back up would be on the other end, waiting for evidence, a confession, or even the key word to come in and rescue him. There was no one! It looked like this was going to be his one last big mistake.

"What I want?" Gordo taunted, and pulled the Glock out of his shoulder holster, turning it over, stroking it lovingly. "What I want is your scalp on a stick. It's for a collection. There's a hefty bounty out for your lovely auburn locks." He glanced over at Lucky. "What'd you do to the kid?"

"Nothing," Arlie said flatly, his brain racing. Should he lie and tell Gordo he had a team waiting or not? Nope, better the man didn't know either way.

"He looks shittier that he normally does. When I saw his Jeep at the egg roll joint, I figured he was just grabbing a bite to eat. Then I saw he had you with him. Or was it you had him? I watched him take you out to Woronzof, sure he was going to call me and turn you over to me there. Or do you in himself. He's never had a kill. Last time we talked, I told him he'd be right up there with the rest of Papa's grandsons if he knocked off someone important. He said he had his reasons for not taking out the judge, but wouldn't say why. We all let it slide, but to stay around himself, he had a deadline."

Gordo laughed again, pointing his gun at the incoherent Lucky then Arlie. "Deadline to get someone dead, get it?" he asked, then laughed again.

"So, Lucky either had to kill me or be killed?"

"Well, not exactly. He could just set you or the judge up, then call me in. You know, deliver the goods. Papa has a soft spot for the kid, him being the oldest grandson and all. The rest of the family was all pretty sure he wasn't blood, but no matter what Papa did, Lucky's mother swore to her last breath that the kid was Alonzo's."

"You mean Papa killed Lucky's mother or you did?" Arlie asked, hoping for a confession, whether it was admissible or not.

"What difference does it make whose hands took her final breath, mine or Papa's? Lucky may be Alonzo's bastard son, but he's still his son. Looks like he's just a runt."

"You asshole!" Lucky shouted, a blur of fists and elbows flailing as he punched and clawed his massive cousin. "You killed my mother!"

Gordo shrugged off the weak-armed attack and threw Lucky into the dark corner, the clatter and jangle of aluminum cans and empty bottles indicating the stoned mama's boy had landed on a pile of bagged trash.

"Your turn," Gordo said, then re-holstered his gun. "I'd scalp you first, Daywalker, just to watch your eyes pop out in shock, but you look like a squirmer to me, not one who'd be paralyzed in shock. I don't want to mess up a good skelping, so I think I'll gut you first. Grabbing your liver, then pulling out your entrails, yard by yard 'til you're dead, makes a big mess, but I won't be the one to clean it up. Besides, if I do this right, Lucky will get the blame. I think your luck just ran out, cousin. You only had a day left, anyhow."

The bulky man finished his fear-inspiring monologue, then lunged. At the flash of shiny metal, Arlie jumped aside, avoiding the nine-inch blade that had suddenly appeared in Gordo's hand. The agile detective thrust with his own knife, trying to knock Gordo's blade away or at least maim his hand so he couldn't hold a weapon.

"Look out!" Lucky screamed from the corner just as Arlie felt the blade penetrate his left side, the scraping sound of metal on rib bone as indescribable as the icy hot pain.

"Ha!" Gordo exclaimed in victory, then stepped back to see how much damage he had inflicted. He tripped on the bucket Arlie had been sitting on and fell backwards to the ground, momentarily stunned.

A moment was enough for Lucky. Still disoriented, he grabbed the fire extinguisher by the door and smashed it into Gordo's face. "That's for Mama!" he screamed, then smashed down again. "And that's for Daywalker, and that's for..."

"Stop," Arlie said weakly. "I need help. A towel or something to stop... Oh, shit. I'm gonna die."

"You're not dead?" Lucky asked, weaving back and forth with the fire extinguisher still in hand.

"Not yet," Arlie said, grasping his gut.

"Oh, shit. Hold on." Lucky grabbed the tee shirt he had doffed while mood swinging and shoved it in Arlie's belly. "Use this 'til I find a towel. Oh, shit. I don't want you to die. Please don't die on me..."

Chapter 9
Cooperation

Due to the uniqueness of Alaska and the broad powers of the United States Marshals Service, deputies in Alaska participate in a variety of special missions. In March 1999, the Alaska Fugitive Task Force was established to pull together resources of several agencies and concentrate apprehension efforts on state and federal fugitives, especially those wanted for crimes of violence and drug trafficking. With the assistance of the Alaska State Troopers, the Anchorage Police Department, the Alaska National Guard Counter-drug Support, the Alaska State Probation/Parole Office and other federal agencies, the Task Force has arrested over 2339 subjects in Alaska and extradited over 100 subjects to other agencies from across the United States. (https://www.usmarshals.gov/district/ak/general/information.htm)

"Hey, Char! Did you get everything you need? It's a good thing Arlie doesn't have a Mini Cooper. We'd have to strap the boys on top!" He walked around the two carts she was standing next to. "Did you leave enough goodies in the store for the next shopper?"

Charlene's mouth spread into a quick, weak smile, then

returned to a concerned frown as she looked past him, searching the store for Arlie.

Just as she brought out her phone, ready to call Arlie's cell again, Marc put his hand on hers. "Don't. He can't answer. I don't know if he told you what you're getting yourself into when he goes undercover, but there is no phone contact. If he calls out, it will be through a third party. They'll get word to you, but you can't talk directly to him."

"Wait. What? I mean, what are you talking about? We were just in here shopping, and now all the sudden he's gone? I was ticked at him, but no good-bye, go to hell, talk to you later?"

"He'd never tell you to go to hell. Shoot, I don't think he'd say that to anyone… No, wait. I can think of a few folks he'd give explicit directions on what to wear and ride while on their way to hell, but you're not one of them. This thing with the De Lucas is getting bad. Really bad from what he says. He saw an opening for a resolution and took it. He asked me to take care of you and the boys. He said Abby will know where he is and if he's dead… I mean, she'll know where he is and how he's doing physically."

"You were right the first time: whether he's dead or

alive."

Marc shrugged his shoulder in admission, then changed the subject. "Oh, and he gave me the keys to his ride. If you'd like, I can take a day or two off and help you get settled." Marc handed her Arlie's keyring and settled into big brother mode. "It's tough being married to a cop. I don't know much about what you've been through since we were in high school together, but I don't think you got softer. I mean," Marc blushed at what could have been construed as a sexual remark, then decided it was best to ignore it. "Well, what I mean is you got tougher when it came to handling life. No one ever pushed Char around, verbally or physically, in the past. I'm sure that tough girl is still ruling, right?"

"Well," Charlene admitted reluctantly, then looked over at the boys and smiled. "A few have tried, and there's a lawsuit still pending on one major league creep, but no, no one's pushed me down or out since the fourth grade. Yes, I'd appreciate it if you helped me load up the car and then followed me to the house and helped me unload. The boys and I can get everything set up or put away after that. There's no need to take time off work. Busying ourselves will help the time pass, too. Please, keep me in the loop."

"Don't worry. I will. You're family now. Even if you aren't married to that rascal yet, you're part of the family of police officers, deputies, and marshals. We take care of our own…and their families."

Chapter 10
How Many Fingers?

A Blue whale carcass washed up on the shore of Newfoundland in 2014. The creature's gigantic heart—440 pounds and the size of a small car—was preserved with the plastination process and at one point was on display as part of The Royal Ontario Museum's Out of the Depths: The Blue Whale Story.

"Judge Taylor?" Arlie whispered hoarsely, his voice dry and raspy. He swallowed, cleared his throat, and tried again. "Judge Taylor? Is that you?"

"Ah, Sleeping Beauty pulls through again. Yes, it's me. I'm glad you're still with the living." He reached towards Arlie's head, grabbed the remote control, then stopped when Arlie touched his hand.

"Not yet. Just you and me first."

"All right, son. What can I do for you?"

Arlie started to laugh, which caused him to cough. One finger up to ask the judge to wait, and he was back in control of his breathing. "Well, first things first. May I have your daughter's hand in marriage? That is, if she still wants to marry me after I went off on an unsanctioned investigation without even letting her know what I was up to."

"Oh, I'm pretty sure she still wants you. Since no man has ever been tough enough to agree to take her on as wife, yes, you have my permission. Looks like you've already agreed to the package deal, too."

"Huh?"

Judge Taylor leaned in close to Arlie's face and looked into his eyes. "You do remember she birthed one son and accepted responsibility for another, right? How many fingers do you see?" he asked and pulled back, holding his clenched fist a foot away from Arlie's face.

"Nine hundred," Arlie answered sarcastically, and shook his head. "Yes, I remember that she's in charge of *my* sons. Not many men get a second chance. Are you sure she's still okay with me?"

"You'll have to ask her yourself. She takes care of the boys mornings and nights, but whenever they're in school, she's here. On the weekends, Lara and I get them while she's camped out here, watching you snore."

"*Weekends*? Crap!" Arlie leaned forward to sit up, then collapsed back. "How long have I been out of it?"

"Nearly six weeks. Charlene said that if you weren't back with the talking walking by Valentine's Day, she was going to knock you out for another six weeks!"

"Six! Weeks?" Arlie asked, his voice and energy strained.

"Here, have a sip of this. They've weaned you off the feeding tube and you've been alert enough to eat food when prompted, but you haven't been lucid until now. You are lucid now, right? Want to try again on how many?" Judge Taylor held up his middle finger, stifling a chuckle.

"One tall bird," Arlie said. "How can I ever make it up to her?"

"Well, I'd say by making a complete recovery."

Arlie looked side to side, overwhelmed with emotional insecurity and physical helplessness, then realized he should be able to ask his future father-in-law anything. "Would you tell me what happened? All I remember is guiding Lucky through an overdose of magic mushrooms," Arlie cleared his throat and licked his lips, trying for composure, and found enough to keep his tears of fear at bay.

He whispered, "Next thing I know, I'm in a hospital bed, can't remember why, and my girlfriend's father is looming over me like he's inspecting me for ticks."

"That would be your *fiancée's* father. You do remember that you just asked me for her hand, right?"

"Yes, I remember. And you said yes, so, please tell me what happened."

"Well, the shorter version is that Gordo popped in on you while you were chatting with Lucky. For some reason, the big guy went ballistic when he saw you, even though you hadn't hurt or done anything to his little cousin. Gordo was trying to decide whether he wanted to scalp you or gut you first when Lucky spoke up for you. You can listen to the playback of the whole thing later. Seems like that handy dandy smartphone of yours does more than just make phone calls. Gordo tossed the scrawny kid against the wall, knocked him senseless, then went after you. That's when you lost your spleen. Or at least he punctured it with a nine-inch blade, messing it up so much the surgeon had to remove it when you got here. But I digress.

"Lucky came after him with a fire extinguisher before he could do more damage to you. Or scalp you. Seems like he has a passion for taking trophies. He left a trail of evidence that will keep the DA busy for months.

"With Gordo conked out and no longer a threat, Lucky grabbed a bath towel, applied pressure to your bleeding gut, and was puking over his shoulder when the paramedics got there. Lucky said he hadn't even had a chance to dial 911 when he heard the ambulances on the way."

"Abby," Arlie said.

"Yup. Your friend Abby was watching your stats from your little custom biometric device, wherever it was you hid it. She had the paramedics ready and around the corner. As soon as your blood pressure dropped, they turned on their sirens and flashers and hit the gas."

"How could she know I was in trouble? There aren't enough emergency vehicles and paramedics for her to have a team standing by twenty-four seven."

"She didn't share her secret and I didn't ask. I have a lot of respect for the gal and her talents. Now, would you like me to call my daughter and tell her you're at least a little bit lucid?"

"No need to do that, Dad. Abby let me know he had left the dazed and confused zone and was back with us in the 'how did I get here from there?' world."

Charlene walked in and kissed Arlie on the forehead.

"How are you feeling, dear?"

"I'm much better, thank you, but you missed." Arlie pointed to his lips.

"No, I didn't. I'll wait to give you a proper hello after you've had a chance to brush your teeth. It's been a while…" Charlene bent over, grinning the whole time she gave her reason, then zeroed in on his lips.

"All right, all right, you two," Judge Taylor said. "I thought you weren't going to kiss him 'til later."

Charlene leaned in and kissed him again, this time quickly. "I couldn't resist."

"So, are you still going to marry me?" Arlie asked. "I mean, just because I've been out of it for a while doesn't mean I forgot about you."

"Sooner or later?" Charlene asked.

"Your choice," he said. "Part of me wants to wait to be legal until I have my strength back, the other part wants you from this minute forth. I'll never stop loving you."

The sound of little boys' feet running down the tile hallway, hollering, "Daddy! Daddy!" interrupted Arlie's soliloquy.

"Sorry," Lara said, herding the boys in front of her. "If I

hadn't kept a firm grip on them, they would have been here five minutes ago. As it was, I let them take the stairs to burn off a little energy. See, I told you your daddy was awake now."

"How many fingers am I holding up," Carlos asked.

"Two," Arlie answered correctly. "What is this, some kind of game?"

"Yeah. Mom and Grandma and Grandpa would let us come in here sometimes to see you. We could talk to you, but you wouldn't answer us. Grandpa said that when you could tell us how many fingers we showed you, you'd be awake!"

"Yeah," Chip added. "And it snowed again last night. Can you come home so we can make a snowman together?"

"Boys, it's going to take a while for your dad to get stronger. We haven't talked to the doctor yet and don't know how long it will be before he can leave here."

"Ah, man!" the boys chorused.

"Yeah, ah, man!" Arlie echoed. "Just let me talk to that man in the silly white coat. Even if he needs to put me in a wheelchair to get me out the door, I'm ready to come home!"

"Yeah, yeah!"

"Did I miss something?" Abby said, as she walked in the room with a large manila envelope and a potted African violet.

"Yes, I'm waiting for an answer from Charlene on how soon she's willing to marry me," Arlie said. "Hey, lady. Thanks for everything you did. I guess I owe you my life."

"Yeah, well, as soon as you're well enough, I'm gonna knock you on your butt for being so reckless. You were and are still on medical leave and not official. That's the only reason you still have a job, but that's a story for later. Thought you'd want to know that you're not going to jail, though, before committing yourself to another kind of life sentence. Good choice on a mate, Charlene. I would have snatched him up long ago if he had been my type," Abby said, adding a wink.

"Well, I'm sure Mimi was glad you were still available when she moved here from North Carolina. You two are such a cute couple," Charlene said.

Abby blushed scarlet, fanned herself with the envelope, then stopped when she remembered what she was holding. "Here, I think this might help you make your decision, Charlene."

Charlene opened the envelope and pulled out a single-paged legal document. "Ah, Arlie. I didn't know you had a chance to send it in…" She brought the marriage license application close for him to see. "Yes, sooner is better. I'll help you recover, whether you're my husband or my fiancé, but I'd rather do it as your wife. I mean, it might make some of our upcoming legal issues easier if we were married."

"Screw legalities," Arlie huffed, then looked up and said, "Sorry 'bout that, Judge."

"No problem," he chuckled as he clutched his grandsons close. "Legal schmeagal is right when it comes to the loving part of family, right boys?"

Charlene grinned at her father, Lara now at his side, enjoying the group hug with their grandsons. *How could she have thought that staying away from their wedding and shunning them was the right thing to do? Ah, giving and receiving second chances were what life was all about.*

"Well, it looks like we have enough witnesses and a judge if you don't mind being in a hospital bed when you say, 'I do.' I mean," Charlene stammered, "I don't mind waiting for the…um…"

Arlie put his hand on hers. "We've waited for the," Arlie

winked instead of assigning an adjective, "part this long, what's a few more days?"

Charlene shifted the envelope to cover the crease in the bedding that might or might not have been a 'happy' tent. When she bumped into the tent pole, she knew it wouldn't be too long and they'd be able to consummate their marriage. "Yes, what's a few more *days* when we'll be together for the rest of our lives?"

"Charlene, my dear, you have the biggest heart in the world."

"Bigger than a Blue whale's?" Carlos asked.

"Big enough to hold all of you in this room," Charlene said.

"And more," Arlie added, looking at her belly which he hoped held more children for them.

"And more," Charlene agreed, patting her womb.

Arlie pushed the remote and sat the bed up to its most vertical position. "We're ready when you are, Judge," he said.

Chapter 11
Time!

According to the wedding industry survey company TheWeddingReport.com, the average couple spends 14 months planning their big day.

"So, we have the paperwork, officiant, witnesses, and desire…" Arlie said with a wink to Charlene. "How long do you think it'll take to whip this impromptu wedding into shape?"

"Is that a challenge?" she asked. "Because I love a challenge. Whether it's to be patient while waiting for my fiancé to come to his full senses or how fast can I throw together a wedding ceremony, I won't back down from a challenge."

Charlene held up an imaginary stopwatch. "Click! Let's get this moving, folks. First, Lara, will you be my matron-of-honor? Oh, and official witness?"

"I'd be honored," Lara said, a blush rising to meet the swelling eyelids that were holding back her tears of joy at complete acceptance by her stepdaughter.

"Abby, would you be the maid-of-honor and the other witness?"

"Well, yeah, but I'm not exactly dressed for it." She looked down at the oversized white government surplus bunny boots and camo-print nylon snow pants she was still wearing. She had been shoveling snow from her driveway when the app on her smartphone signaled her that Arlie's brainwave activity indicated he was having a conversation. There was no way she was going to stop and change before coming to verify it! "Ah, what the heck. Maybe I'll start a trend."

"Boys, since this is a two-ring ceremony, you both get to hold a ring, all right?"

"Yeah, yeah!"

"Two rings?" Arlie asked. "I didn't even get a chance to buy yours…"

"So?" Charlene shrugged a shoulder. "You'd let me pick out whatever I wanted, right?"

Arlie nodded, started to speak, then decided that this shouldn't be an argument, and any comments would be wasted energy. He'd shut up so the ceremony would come together quicker.

"And since I wanted them to be similar, I picked out yours at the same time. I took your old college class ring to the jeweler and he sized it. Bret said if it didn't fit, he could modify it. Oh, and I forgot to tell you, I've been taking care of your day-to-day responsibilities while you slumbered in recovery. Your mailbox key was on the keyring for the Hummer, so I've been paying your bills. Oh, and taking care of all other incoming letters and packages," she said, and added a big smirk, letting him know that all the cash they had mailed had been received and was safely stashed.

"The boys and I got a family car—another Subaru. It's kind of like the one I had in Arizona, but this one has all the bells, whistles, heated seats, and follow-the-steering headlights. It's white, too, so we aren't high visibility like the old ride. I didn't want to call too much attention to us now, did I?"

"You did sell it, or at least use the Hummer as a trade-in, right?"

Charlene shook her head. "Nope. I couldn't do either since I'm not on the title. But I did rent it out to the Alaska foster care folks for a buck a month. They can use it for in-town transportation, to take kids sledding or ice-fishing—

whatever a situation requires. I told them to go ahead and put fancy decals on it, so it's also a drive around billboard asking for folks to volunteer to be foster parents."

"And it's no longer a traveling target for bad guys looking for me?"

"Yup. Looks like your brain's still working just fine. Now, I think we have it all together," Charlene said, looking around to see if she was missing something.

"How about flowers?" Abby asked.

"You already brought them to Arlie," Charlene said, lifting the little foil-wrapped potted plant. "See, not only is the container blue, but so are the frilly little African violets. And since these are his, I'll have something both borrowed and something blue."

"And they're new and old at the same time," Arlie added. "They're new to me, but the plant's old, or sort of. At least, it's not a seedling or a cutting. Then it would be new."

"Something old, something new; something borrowed, something blue. I think that's about all we need," Judge Taylor said.

"Not quite," Lara said. "I think the boys and I have one more surprise. Come on, guys. We have a little chit chatting to do with a friend."

Lara left the room with the boys chanting, "Bye, Dad. See ya, Dad," as the judge scrolled through files on his smartphone. "I know I have it somewhere… Oh, here it is. I found it. The perfect wedding vows. Or at least I thought so. They're the ones I wrote for my marriage to Lara. You can use them, if you'd like. Just swap out the names."

"I'm so sorry I didn't go, Dad," Charlene said. "I was a jerk."

"Well, yes you were. But you've apologized and shown remorse, and we're all back on track—the most wonderful family in the world. Or at least one of them." He wrapped his arms around her and gave her a big, rocking-back-and-forth bear hug, like she was a toddler. "No sadness allowed on your wedding day. Daddy's orders. I'd say judge's orders, but my daddy suit trumps my judge's robes in this situation."

"Thanks, Dad.

"Hey, Charlene, do you want to come outside with me for a few?" Abby asked. "I'm getting hot in these clothes and could use some fresh air."

Abby herded Charlene out the door, then turned back and winked at the judge. "Your turn," she whispered to him.

"Hi. Sorry to interrupt," the nurse said to Arlie, "but I need to take your stats. I can get you a pain pill if you need one, but by your smile, I trust your lady's standing order of nothing more than Ibuprofen stands."

"Yes, it seems my fiancée did a great job of conveying my wishes." Arlie scooted up and changed positions. "Actually, I don't feel too bad. I thought I'd be a shriveled-up bag of bones after being out of it for so long."

"You can thank your physical therapist for that," the nurse said, then stuck the thermometer in his mouth. "You had workouts twice a day. This fancy bed tips all the way upright so your circulation and weight-bearing muscles stayed in shape. She moved you around in familiar ways, too—lifting your arms up like brushing your hair, eating—that sort of thing." She took his wrist and glanced at her watch as she checked his pulse. "Nice and steady. Strong, too. It's amazing how much difference being able to carry on a conversation makes. You've been eating and using the bathroom as prompted for weeks now. I'd ask how many fingers do I have, but I think you've moved beyond that now. Is there anything you need?"

Arlie frowned, reminding her he still had the probe in his

mouth. "Oops!" She took it out. "Normal. Now is there anything I can do for you?"

"Yes, call the doctor and see how soon I can get out of this hospital!"

"Sure, except you're not in a hospital. You're in Chugach Extended Care. I'll check with him and get back to you," the nurse said, then left the room.

"So, I'm in an old folks home? Shoot, I'm not even thirty and in a nursing home." Arlie chuckled. "Beat you there, Judge!"

"It wasn't a race, but I'm glad you'll be leaving soon. You got the best care available, Charlene saw to that."

"Yeah, she's a keeper, for sure. So, now that everyone else is gone, what happened to Lucky?"

"Well, after the medics checked him out and he recovered from his intestinal distress, he asked to speak to me. Said he didn't want any old lawyer, just me. When he was told I wasn't available, he said he'd not say a word to anyone until I was. Turns out he was happy to be incarcerated. Never said a lick to anyone until I came back from Hawaii. I came in and talked to him and got an earful. He agreed to tell all on everyone in the family in exchange for immunity and inclusion in the witness protection program. I'm not sure where he is now, but I do know one thing."

"What's that, Judge?"

"He said being a red head wasn't all that bad, and as soon as he was out, he was getting a buzz cut and letting himself go natural. I pulled down the neck of my shirt and showed him the red hairs on my chest and winked at him. Told him both my grandsons were red heads, too."

"And their father," Arlie said. "But that's another story for another day."

"We got it!" Lara said. "The boys and I have the cafeteria reserved for the wedding reception. We can either have it at ten or two, before or after lunch. Which one do you prefer?"

"Duh! The sooner the better: ten o'clock! Oh, by the way, what time is it now?" Arlie asked, rubbing his chin. "And do I have time for a shave?" He pulled his pajama top away from his chest. "And maybe a shower and a change of clothes?"

Judge Taylor looked at his watch. "It's almost nine."

"I'll let the cook know we're doing the early shift. Come on, boys," Lara said, urging her grandsons out of the room again. "Your dad needs to get spruced up a little."

Judge Taylor shut the door behind them. "I'll help you

with the shower."

Arlie frowned, embarrassed that he needed assistance.

"It won't be the first time I helped, but I'm sure it'll be the last," he said, and turned on the shower. "I just get the water ready, soap up the washcloth, and stand by in case you fall off the shower seat." The Judge stood back as Arlie swung his legs over the bed, testing his feet before walking into the bathroom.

"As the nurse said, you've been doing lots of tasks for a couple weeks, although bathing has only been for the last few days. I'm sure there's a razor around somewhere, but I think Charlene likes that rugged and ragged look, so you might take that into consideration. Then, after you've dried off, I have a surprise for you."

"Can we skip the wait?" Arlie called out from the shower. "*Everything* is a surprise to me today."

"All right. I sneaked in a nice suit for you last week. It's in your closet. Charlene doesn't know you'll be dressed to the nines. I think that's why Abby pulled her out of here, too. We both know neither of them are girly girls, but Abby insisted she be allowed to dress Charlene if I was going to dress you."

"Whoa. Wait. So this impromptu wedding has been planned…"

"No, not really. Abby and Charlene read a lot of wedding magazines while waiting for you to recover. Abby just took what she'd learned about Charlene's tastes, took a leap of faith, and had the gown made. She shared her plan with me, so I was responsible for a suit for you. It was no secret you two were getting married. It was just a matter of when. All of us wanted to be prepared. I was an Eagle Scout, too, you know."

Arlie accepted the suit, looked it over with a grunt of acceptance, then looked back in the closet. "Is this all there is?"

"Why, yes…"

"Then I guess I'll either get married barefoot or with slippers, depending on how cold the floor is."

Knock. Knock.

"We're ready if you are," Abby said. "All we need is a groom and the room."

Judge Taylor opened the door. "Well, I thought I had everything. Looks like I forgot to get shoes."

"Well, looks like you're not alone. I forgot, too," Abby

said. She stepped aside. "So, what do you think of the barefoot bride?"

Charlene walked forward. "There's no way anything white could be as beautiful as this. I don't think there's even a word to describe the color."

Arlie opened his mouth to speak, then saw the awe on everyone's faces as she walked forward. *Don't tell her it's the color Lucky called Cold Weenie Purple!* "Aurora borealis violet," he said. "Perfect."

***

Wedding vows, rings, and kisses were exchanged in Arlie's small but adequate room, then the party proceeded to the dining room, the groom seated in the hastily adorned wheelchair, the clatter, clatter of the playing cards clipped to the wheel spokes announcing his arrival to the two dozen other residents of the recovery facility. Some wore street clothes, others were in robes and pajamas, a few had eyes glistening with happy tears, but all sported wide smiles.

"Congratulations, Officer Biggar," the facility's chef said. "I'd have baked a cake for you, had I known, but Lara and the boys said this will do."

"Best Wishes" was spelled out in raisins on top of a huge

pan of bread pudding. "I couldn't fit 'congratulations' on it with raisins, and I didn't have any decorating tips, so…" The chef shrugged his shoulder. "At least, they tell me this is your favorite dessert, so that part worked out."

"There have been bigger and fancier weddings, I'm sure," Arlie said. "Probably more elaborate receptions, too, but nothing beats what my friends and family have done for me today. I am, without a doubt, the happiest man on earth. Oh, and I think I've finally learned to trust, too." Arlie squeezed Charlene's hand at his shoulder.

"Here's to the bride and groom," Judge Taylor said, his glass of cranberry juice raised in a toast, "And to love and trust, hope and faith, health and peace."

"Here, here," Arlie said, answering his toast. "Everything else is just stuff!"

The End of this story

The beginning of a new life

A Note from the Author

Thank you for reading THE BIGGEST HEART EVER, the second book in the ARLIE UNDERCOVER series. Book Three in the series, ALWAYS A BIGGER FISH, is available now.

If you enjoyed this story, I would appreciate it if you'd help others know a bit about it, too. Others will find your reading experience helpful when deciding if this is a book for them. Please leave a review on Amazon, BookBub and/or Goodreads.

Other books by Dani Haviland

A Stingray Christmas: (First book in the Arlie Undercover series) Anchorage detective on medical leave travels from Alaska to Arizona to see for the first time the son he'd fathered as an anonymous sperm donor. Great and rotten surprises await the cop with the smartest smartphone around.

Always a Bigger Fish: (Book three in the Arlie Undercover series) Arlie is hoping for a boring caseload after recovering from a stabbing wound that nearly took his life, but an intimidating package has just arrived at the forensics department. It seems that someone is out to take his and his US Deputy Marshal buddy's scalps.

THE FAIRIES SAGA SERIES

(in order with novellas):

Naked in the Winter Wind: (lengthy novel) How does an older woman wind up as a young hottie in Revolutionary War era North Carolina? First book in the time travel series.

Ha'Penny Jenny: (historical novella) More about the naïve and psychic young girl who was adopted into a time traveling family. Will her past catch up to her?

Aye, I am a Fairy: (lengthy novel) Young British lord finds himself entwined with a time traveling family and must decide if he should go back in time, too. Second book in the series.

Dances Naked: (novel) Directionally challenged time traveler is rescued by Cherokee in 18th century. What must he do before the chief will show him to The Trees, the portal through time?

Chasing Christmas: (historical novella) A young Cherokee is rescued from an abusive man and changes the lives of many in this 18th century America family.

The Great Big Fairy: (lengthy novel) Very tall Benji grew up in the 20th century but was born in the 18th. When he finds a way to return to his grandparents in the distant past, he goes for it. Once there, he realizes he can't stay, but must return to the future. Fourth book in the series.

Little Drummer Boy: (historical novella) Young Scout works to earn money for a home in post-Revolutionary War America but runs up against prejudices and snowstorms.

Never Too Young: (historical novella) Scout and Ha'Penny Jenny have grown up, but will they be able to spend their life together, or will the past and ruffians get in their way?

Time in a Little Blue Bottle: Mark Twain, Elvis, the prime vampire Cleveland, and time traveler Marty Melbourne help two youths thwart the bad guys who are out to steal Fountain of Youth water.

CONTEMPORARY NOVELLAS

Benji: The Early Years

Luke the Unexpected: Love of classic motorcycles brought them together, but Luke and Holly have other challenges to face. Find out how their friend Benji got his stripes here.

Pool Boy Wanted: No Experience Preferred: (rather racy) Young Benji has been a hostage and slave, but life gets worse when an older woman decides she wants him as her own.

STAND ALONE NOVELLAS

Kit Kringle: An Alaskan Tale: (contemporary) Kay moved to Alaska for the wrong reasons, then decided to stay and start her own business. What she hadn't planned on were prejudices and falling in love.

Be My Angel: (contemporary) The love of horses brought them together. Could a greedy woman break them apart?

Three Are One: (contemporary) Kizzie's husband shunned their special needs daughter and volunteered for Iraq to avoid his family and engage in nefarious operations that ended in his death. The post chaplain tried to help the young widow adjust, but would his feelings for her and the search for his lost sister cause problems?

One Arctic Summer: (contemporary) The touch she never forgot.

 Dani Haviland has never been one to believe, "You can't do that!" She started her own business in 1994, selling tractor parts in Alaska, then segued to writing and publishing books, becoming a *USA Today* bestselling author in the process. She currently splits her time between Alaska and Oregon, tirelessly writing and gardening, publishing and promoting, while claiming to be 'retired.'

Contact

Dani Haviland can be found at:

Amazon Author page: http://bit.ly/dhAuthor

Newsletter sign up: http://bit.ly/2DHnews

Website: http://bit.ly/DaniHaviland

Twitter: https://twitter.com/dani_haviland

Facebook: https://www.facebook.com/dani.haviland

BookBub: http://bit.ly/BBDani

Goodreads Author page: http://bit.ly/2DHgdrds

www.ingramcontent.com/pod-product-compliance
Lightning Source LLC
Chambersburg PA
CBHW080840250626
47161CB00009B/3140